WITCH'S
BREW
IN
THE PEW

Dr. Drew Rousse
with David Alsobrook

FOREWORD BY DAVID ALSOBROOK

Witch's Brew in the Pew, by Dr. Drew Rousse with
David Alsobrook
ISBN # 0-89228-085-9
Copyright ©, 2000 by Impact ChristianBooks, Inc.
    Original Copyright ©, 1997 by Drew Rousse.
    First Printing - June, 1997

Published by
Impact Christian Books, Inc.
332 Leffingwell Ave.,
Kirkwood, MO 63122
314-822-3309

Cover Design: *Ideations*

Table of Contents

FOREWORD

"At the next campmeeting we're having Drew Rousse!" The crowd broke into spontaneous applause. "Remember the little girl who was healed at the last meeting? Be sure and bring anyone who needs a miracle. This brother is one ragin' Cajun!"

After the meeting I went up to the camp director and asked, "Who is this brother?" Mrs. Miller looked at me with her famous big eyes, made all the bigger because of her magnifying glasses, and asked incredulously, "Do you mean to tell me you don't know Drew Rousse?" "Sorry, I guess I'm behind the times." "Well," she stated, "He's an anointed person." I love to be around people who are greatly used of God, so I inquired about Drew's ministry, address, and schedule.

Over the years I've heard many "Drew stories" in my travels. A "Drew story" inevitably has some miraculous event in it which occurred in a regular type meeting which transformed it into a memorable one. Hundreds of people have found healing for body, mind, and spirit through Brother Rousse's incredible faith and anointing. The church he and his capable wife lead, is full of enthusiastic believers whose lives have been changed and enriched. God is always glorified whenever Drew ministers.

One of Brother Rousse's gifts is "sing-preaching." I'll never forget the first time I heard Drew exercise this gift. I was driving down the highway with one of his tapes playing. Suddenly Drew's voice took on a musical quality, and he began to sing his sermon with cadences rising and falling. I looked down at my arms and saw goose-bumps covering them. I felt an impartation of the very faith of God into my spirit and was blessed.

Dr. Rousse has invited me to fill his pulpit several times. I've always left his church feeling that I had received more than I had given. Once I approached him and asked, "Brother Rousse, would you lay hands on me and impart the gift of faith?" He did so, and I was strengthened in my inner man at once.

Drew's ministry takes him outside the country and often puts him on radio and television. His simple messages, enlivened by the anointing, impart strength and hope into the hearts of the hearers. Jesus is exalted, and people are drawn to Him.

Wanda is a unique blessing to her husband. She is a woman of many talents and giftings. Together, the Rousse's make an unbeatable team.

In this book, composed of several of Dr. Rousse's sermons, you will discover an insight into witchcraft in the church, one of the enemy's more subtle workings.

Open your heart and mind to the truths you are about to discover, and let the truth set you free from *the witch's brew.*

David Alsobrook
Nashville, Tennessee

ENDORSEMENTS

"Witch's Brew in the Pew," the title of this book will have positive or negative effects on Church leaders as they glance around the Christian Book shop. Those leaders who will digest every word of it will be those who know that little foxes are spoiling the vines and are affecting fruitfulness in the Church. Church leaders who know that even to approach such a can of worms will have drastic repercussions, will avoid it. However, one never finds flies around a place which is fully disinfected, so the Lord of the Flies (Satan) will not breed around such spiritual disinfectant as this book.

Dr. Eric Belcher
Christ for the Nations

God hath done it again! He has given us another classic through my dear friend, Bishop Drew Rousse. After 44 years of preaching the Gospel, I am so delighted God has raised up an author to "tell it like it is." *The Witch's Brew in The Pew* is certainly overdue; it has been so desperately needed down through the years to handle the "space cadets" who fly through the local church. God has been so good to our author. Bishop Rousse has an insight like no other I know. I would like to say this book is not one you will lay down and forget. You will read it over and over again, and pass it to your friends. At times it could be controversial, but when you read it with an open heart, you will see that the church is more victorious than we have thought—for we are more than conquerors through Christ Jesus!

The Reverend Dr. Jerry B. Walker

*Every now and then, a book is written that people can't wait to get their hands on. **Witch's Brew in the Pew** is that type of book.*

It was on the National as well as the internationally known Trinity Broadcasting Network that this insightful book was introduced to the world.

While my wife and I were hosting the ever popular Praise The Lord Program, we introduced to the world for the first time this author and his book whose seasons have come.

The response to the interview was phenomenal! There were many calls and letters requesting copies of this book.

We believe this book is destined to be a best seller!

We commend you, Dr. Drew Rousse, for a job well done.

Dr. Beau Williams

Recording Artist --Evangelist—Producer --Songwriter — Vocal Coach

Chapter 1

WHAT IS WITCHCRAFT?

Is someone practicing witchcraft on you?

That may sound like a strange question. After all, it would be obvious that someone was casting a spell over you, if that person rode a broom and wore a funny black hat. Witches don't look that way anymore, especially witches in the church.

Paul asked the Galatians to identify the person(s) who had cast a spell on them: *O foolish Galatians! Who has bewitched you that you should not obey the truth...?* (Galatians 3:1, NKJV). Notice that Paul did not ask them, *if* they had been bewitched, but rather asked them, *who* it was who had done this thing. I'm sure none of them had even thought of the possibility.

Many of you who are reading this book have been directed to it by the prompting of the Holy Spirit. The witch's brew in the pew is a state of trouble or strain, a compelling force or influence of a negative nature that touches the life of a Christian, because of physical or spiritual contact with an unclean thing. He wants to reveal that you have a "witch's brew" over you through the revelation of His Word within these pages. Jesus declared, "You shall know the truth and the truth shall make you free" (John 8:32).

I decree to you, in Jesus' Name, a time of victory over witchcraft. God is going to break the spirit of witchcraft over you as you have the faith to believe Him through the hearing of His Word (Ro 10:17).

Through the truth in this book you are going to be made free from the curse of witchcraft!

Jesus was made a curse for us when He hung on the Cross, *"for curseth is He that hangeth on a tree,"* (Galatians 3:13). We have power through His Blood to use His Name and tear down the walls of witchcraft by the power of the Holy Spirit. Satan assigns spirits of witchcraft intending for them to destroy the children of God. But, like every other weapon he forms against us, this one, too, comes to nothing (Isaiah 54:17).

Jezebel Introduced

In a later section we will study an ancient queen in Israel whose name was Jezebel. She controlled her husband by the spirit of witchcraft and through controlling her weak husband, King Ahab, she was able to exert immense control over Israel.

Jezebel was referred to by our ascended King, the glorified Lord Jesus, in one of His messages to the seven churches of Asia. Let's look at His reproof:

> [18] *And unto the angel of the church in Thyatira write; These things saith the Son of God, who hath his eyes like unto a flame of fire, and his feet are like fine brass;*
> [19] *I know thy works, and charity, and service, and faith, and thy patience, and thy works; and the last to be more than the first.*

20 Notwithstanding I have a few things against thee, because thou sufferest that woman Jezebel, which calleth herself a prophetess, to teach and seduce my servants to commit fornication, and to eat things sacrificed unto idols.

21 And I gave her a space to repent of her fornication; and she repented not.

22 Behold, I will cast her into a bed, and them that commit adultery with her into great tribulation, except they repent of their deeds.

23 And I will kill her children with death; and all the churches shall know that I am he which searcheth the reins and hearts: and I will give unto every one of you according to your works.

24 But unto you I say, and unto the rest in Thyatira, as many as have not this doctrine, and which have not known the depths of Satan, as they speak; I will put upon you none other burden.

25 But that which you have already hold fast till I come.

26 And he that overcometh, and keepeth my works unto the end, to him will I give power over the nations.

27 And he shall rule them with a rod of iron; as the vessels of a potter shall they be broken to shivers: even as I received of my Father.

28 And I will give him the morning star.

29 He that hath an ear, let him hear what the Spirit saith unto the churches."

Revelation 2:18-29

Witchcraft Defined

Witchcraft comes from the original word *kashaph* and means *to whisper a spell, speak a curse, practice magic.* Witchcraft can be separated into two cate-gories: white and black.

White witchcraft refers to the delusion some witches are under as they believe they are using Satan's power to affect mankind for good. Black witches understand that their sorceries, spells, and incantations are intended to bring evil on the objects of their bewitchments.

The Brew Principal

Sometimes witches (both white and black) attend churches in order to emit the powers of the evil one over the congregation. They often target the leadership of the church in order to bring the whole ministry down. Back at their covens they attempt to cast spells on the various ones they target. After initial contact they no longer need to attend the church in order to exert influence. They can spew their brew from a distance. One thing leaders should understand is that you can have a witch's brew in the pew without having the witch present. The witch can send the "brew." It can be in the pew, and on you, without anyone being aware of it.

The woman Christ identified as "Jezebel" in the above text, however, *was present* in the local congregation at Thyatira. In fact, she occupied a position of leadership, or at least a position of influence, in that church. She represents the most common problem in churches today, especially Full Gospel, Word of Faith, Holy Ghost filled churches.

An individual whom everyone knows and respects as a devout Christian exerts a position of control or influence over individuals in the fellowship and turns them away from the leadership of that church causing dissension, criticism, and eventual division from within. He or she rarely knows they are tools of Satan to actually hinder and even destroy the work of God in their community. Like Jesus' first disciples they do not know what "manner of spirit" they are of (Luke 9:55).

Identifying the Brew

Let me present some of the identifying marks of the witch's brew to help identify someone in your church who may be concocting a brew against you:

1.   Excessive control:
This is obvious when an individual attempts to exercise too much authority over others, holding them back to an extreme degree, and keeping them down beyond reason. Sometimes the leadership in a church gets in the wrong spirit and usurps the personal lordship of Christ over a believer.

Witchcraft in a church can operate from beneath or above, but those under an excessively controlling pastor should not speak against him. They should pray for him, lovingly appeal to him, and then, if no change occurs, quietly leave that church and seek a pastor who uses his authority wisely and with love. Most witchcraft in the church today comes from beneath.

2.   Manipulation:
This occurs when one changes the function of another for one's own purpose or advantage; treats unfairly or dishonestly. This is a problem in homes when a wife, for instance, may seek to usurp the headship of her husband when he makes a decision which she doesn't like.

3.   Threats:

Witchcraft spirits issue statements of possible harm or evil. I have seen this occur in ministries when persons of considerable financial assets threaten to leave the church if they do not get their way. Pastors frequently submit to the "purse strings" of well-to-do parishioners and quench the Spirit in their churches.

4.   Violations of Rule:

This can best be summed up by the term *law breaker.* In Thyatira Jezebel taught God's servants to commit immorality and participate in idol worship. The witch's brew eventually leads to gross sin. Many a man of God has been pulled down by a woman operating under the influence of this spirit in the local church. This spirit begins its influence by compromising clear standards.

5.   Refusal to Submit to Authority:

One of the characteristics of the Wilderness Generation was rebellion. The children of Israel frequently murmured against the leadership of Moses and were destroyed because of their stiff-necked rebellion against his authority.

How Do You Stack Up?

Look at each of these trademarks slowly and let me ask the question once again, "Is someone practicing witchcraft on you?" Allow the Holy Spirit to reveal any brew operating over you. If you are still unsure you might want to go to Chapter Four right now and study the twenty-four characteristics of witchcraft.

Whether or not, he or she realizes it, anyone operating under the influence of witchcraft, is a Jezebel. In the next chapter we will look at Jezebel more closely by examining her influence over Ahab, and through Ahab, over Israel. Jezebel even exerted influence over the prophet Elijah, one of the greatest men of God in the Scriptures. Is it any wonder many men of God areso influenced today?

Chapter 2

THE JEZEBEL SPIRIT

In I Kings Chapter 18 we are given the account of the Elijah/Baal confrontation on Mt. Carmel. It was there that the mighty prophet challenged the false prophets of Baal—that the God who "answered by fire" would be the true God whom Israel would serve rather than halting between two opinions. It was a tense moment on the popular mountain when Elijah issued his challenge. Lets take a closer look:

> 31 *And Elijah took twelve stones, according to the number of the tribes of the sons of Jacob, unto whom the word of the Lord came, saying, Israel shall be thy name.*
> 38 *Then the fire of the Lord fell, and consumed the burnt sacrifice, and the wood, and the stones, and the dust, and licked up the water that was in the trench.*
> 39 *And when all the people saw it, they fell on their faces: and they said, The Lord, he is the God; the Lord, he is the God.*
> 40 *And Elijah said unto them, Take the prophets of Baal; let not one of them escape. And they took them: and Elijah brought them down to the brook Kishon, and slew them there.*
>
> 1Kings 18:31,38-40

Pay particular attention to the word "twelve stones." Each stone represented a tribe of Israel, but there is more to it than that. Twelve is representative of the number of government or authority. **Witchcraft always challenges governmental authority**.

Elijah had great power with God and performed many miracles. He raised the dead, called down fire, killed 450 Baal prophets and ate food supernaturally provided by ravens. The Spirit of the Lord was upon him to such a degree that he even controlled the weather. Elijah declared that "there will not be dew nor rain but by my word" and altered the weather patterns in Israel for $3\frac{1}{2}$ years! Elijah moved in super-natural physical strength. He not only slew 450 false prophets single-handedly, but for twenty miles he outran the king's chariot, because the Spirit of the Lord was upon him (see 1Kg 17,18). What a mighty man of God! Surely he would never fear anybody or anything! Right? Wrong!

As mighty as Elijah was, and as great as his anointing was, the simple fact of the matter is that he ran away from a woman who threatened his life. Elijah had received many threats before and had never been afraid. After all, God was with him in an amazing way. Yet, when an ungodly woman issued a challenge to him, he feared for his life and ran away to a desolate mountain. This was the greatest failure of his life, because had Elijah remained with the populace, he could have capitalized on the miracles of the fire and rain the day before, and called the whole nation to repentance and to destruction of all the idols. Instead, he ran away, because he allowed a spirit to operate over him during a weak moment. This is not only true of Elijah, but of many men and women of God who have been suppressed, controlled, and driven from the center of God's will by means of the witch's brew operating through a modern day Jezebel.

Consider Your Life Today

Perhaps you are a real Christian, filled with the Spirit of God. Your confidence usually rides high, but today, you are cowering under the influence of a witchcraft spirit. You are under strong control, yet you have great confidence in God. You believe God can do anything. You believe God is a God of miracles. Yet, your confidence is shattered. What did it take to break your confidence?

If I were to tell you that it might be a "witch's brew in the pew" seeking to break your confidence, would you be willing to believe me?

The Jezebel Brew

Jezebel was a witch, even though she was a queen over God's covenant people. This witch sent her brew to Elijah through a messenger, not even in person, and all the messenger said to Elijah was, "If you are still alive at this time tomorrow...", and Elijah fled for his life! (1Kings 19:2). After he ran a great distance, Elijah curled up under a juniper tree (a spreading broom tree which offered shade from the sun). He napped awhile and awoke when an angel visited him and fed him. He ate and slept again, only to be awakened once more and instructed to eat again, because the journey before him was great. He went in the strength of that heavenly prepared meal for forty days until he came to Horeb, the Mount of God, where Elijah, who still felt sorry for himself, received a new commission from God (1Kings 19:5).

The question remains. What would change a man of faith into a man of cowardice? What could possibly cause a man of God who stood up against 450 prophets, who raised the dead, who stopped and started the rain and dew, who ran in front of the fastest chariot to turn into a whimpering, whining individual filled with self-pity and dread? What could do that? **A WITCH'S BREW, that's what!**

The Brew and You

It is important that we must recognize the fact that if this witch's brew could have this kind of effect over Elijah then, it could do the same thing to any one of us. After all, James says that Elijah was "a man of like passions" as ourselves (James 5:17). If Elijah was susceptible, then we are too. I suggest for your consideration that some of the feelings that you have had and some of the decisions you have made may very well been the result of the "witch's brew" on you.

Let me ask you some more questions:

- **Are you going through great times of discouragement?**
- **Are you bound by a terrible fear?**
- **Are you seeing terrible things all around you?**
- **Have you felt your confidence in God shaken to the core of your being?**

There may be a witch's brew being practiced on you. Nervous conditions are often the product of a witch's brew. People, who cannot get a handle on their emotions and experience great mood swings from which they plunge on into depression, are often under the spell of a witch's brew.

All across America thousands of people have left churches in which God placed them, because of the effects of witchcraft being practiced on them. We are in a real war. Paul said it this way, "You are not warring against flesh and blood but against principalities and powers, the rulers of darkness of this world, spiritual wickedness in heavenly places..." (Ephesians 6:12).

Do you realize that many ministries have been pulled down because of a witch's brew? Some of the tele- evangelists who had worldwide ministries drank of the witch's brew and are now dissolved. How could witchcraft have this kind of power over a child of God?

The Brew of Deception

I believe with all my heart that the biggest power that Satan has, in the sense of witchcraft, is what we see in the Garden. I refer, of course, to *deception* (Genesis 3:1). Deception operated only under the cover of darkness. Preachers who will not put light on the devil, showing him for what he is, are taking a chance of being destroyed by the witch's brew. We are called to put light on the devil.

The Bible tells us that when the light shines in the darkness, the darkness cannot grab hold, nor comprehend it (John 1:5).

Let the light of the Word coming to you from these pages penetrate the darkness you may be under right now and be liberated from the witch's brew! Of course, often a problem is multi-faceted and has many roots. We are now going to look at the root of witchcraft.

Chapter 3

THE ROOT OF WITCHCRAFT

The Brew of Rebellion

Witchcraft is the unlawful art of imposing one's will over another. A person under the spell of witchcraft may want to do one thing but ends up doing it another way, often experiencing a change of heart about persons in lawful positions of authority. A believer who comes under witchcraft always ends up in rebellion. This is what witchcraft is all about. It is always associated with rebellion (1Samuel 15:23). The primary reason this is so is because when Lucifer rebelled he fell and became Satan, the adversary, and his greatest efforts all revolve around aligning mankind in his rebellion against God and all godly authority. He uses witchcraft to control people and get them to do things contrary to God's will.

The Cain Brew

The first time witchcraft was exposed in the worship of God is seen in Genesis, chapter four. Cain and Abel were offering their sacrifices to the Lord "in process of time" (v. 3). Witchcraft began to work through Cain, when he became very jealous of his brother Abel. Even though Abel was the second son, God had posi tioned him in spiritual authority over Cain because he was a shepherd—the one in charge of the flock. In a sense, Cain would have to humble himself to go to Abel for a lamb to sacrifice.

God had previously shown man, through the coats of skins in the Garden, that the only way to push sin forward was through the offering of a BLOOD SACRIFICE. Cain had no ability to offer a blood sacrifice, because he was a tiller of the ground (a farmer). This necessitated his going to his brother, Abel, and exchanging what his hands had produced (crops) in order to procure a lamb for a blood sacrifice. This should have been no problem at all, but what is inferred, is that Cain did not like the idea of submitting to his younger brother. Cain became jealous and angry. The final product of that witch's brew is that he killed his brother. He killed the one who was put in authority over him **by God.**

There are saints of God today who are being killed by their brothers because of jealousy and rebellion to authority.

Sometimes Christians use the Word of God to chop their brothers and sisters to death. Others go out of their way to teach certain things which bring confusion and fear to immature Christians who, in turn, become "missing in action" because they leave church altogether, filled with mistrust. Many people in our day do not know whom they can trust as a spiritual leader because the devil has painted the picture that preachers are filled with lusts of various kinds and have ulterior motives. It is often said that all preachers are interested in, is other men's wives and money.

The witch's brew has spread these lies to the body of Christ for the purpose of breaking down the faith, trust, and confidence within the hearts of God's people toward the men and women of God. When the devil can bring in doubt, he can then introduce unbelief. Unbelief kept the children of Israel out of the Promised Land and keeps many believers from inheriting their place of rest in God as well (Hebrews 3:19).

There is another facet about jealousy that we need to consider at this point. It is vitally important that we understand just how dangerous and destructive jealousy can be, because, as James puts it, *"Where there is envying and strife, there is every evil work"* (James 3:16). If the devil can separate God's people, and bring mistrust among them toward God's ministers, he then has established a beachhead in the local church. He has an opening, through which to spew his brew to the pew. Whenever anyone listens to the voice of Satan whisper-ing the witch's brew into his spiritual ear, he or she takes those thoughts into the mind, which, if not stopped, enter the heart and diminish faith. We begin to allow the devil to take control of our thoughts and reasoning processes, the next thing that happens, is that we fall out of faith and into doubt and unbelief.

Cain rebelled against *God's designated authority*, murdering his own brother and spending the rest of his life wandering and in confusion. Witchcraft tries to dominate the spiritual realm. Witchcraft fights designated authority. Witchcraft seeks to destroy spiritual leaders and always, in the final analysis, destroys the one who practices it as well. (Jezebel, you will recall, was thrown out of her palace window onto the street below, where the dogs lapped up her blood! Jesus promised the Jezebel at Thyatira a bed of pain and death for her children [followers] if they continued to rebel.)

The root of witchcraft is rebellion against spiritual authority.

Chapter 4

TWENTY-FIVE
CHARACTERISTICS
OF WITCHCRAFT

In this chapter I want to provide an exhaustive list of witchcraft characteristics. The more we know about the workings of the enemy, the better we can assail him.

1.   Witchcraft works through rebellion against authority and refuses to submit to God's designated authority the earth.

In Mark, chapter one, we read of an occasion when an unclean spirit operated through a man right in the middle of a worship service. Jesus, unmoved by the disturbance, cast the spirit out of the man.

The Holy Spirit operated through the ministry of Jesus in great power and blessing. The Messiah did not teach like one of the Pharisees or Scribes, but He taught as "one having authority" (Mark 1:22). As Jesus spoke the Word in authority, immediately from the depths of one listener's soul, from the back of that synagogue, an unclean spirit screamed out, "What have You to do with us, Jesus of Nazareth? Have You come to torment us? Have You come to destroy us? We know who You are, the Holy One of God!" Jesus said, "Be muzzled, gagged, and come out of him." The man was thrown on the ground and the demon came out of that individual. What did the rest of the church say that day? "We've never seen this before" (Mark 1:27, *paraphrased*).

What does the Lord want us to learn from this event? I believe one lesson is that God's designated authority, as expressed by Jesus, has power over the authority of Satan. Your Heavenly Father wants you to know, child of God, that He who lives inside you is greater than the ruler of this world (1John 4:4). Satan's power is limited. If he was able to have his way, he would have destroyed you a long time ago. It is not his plan that you came to Jesus, nor does he like it, that you are reading this book right now.

God has placed this book in your hands so you can gain more knowledge of the evil one, and see him defeated in your life. The truths in this volume will keep him at bay. The enemy will not defeat you, in fact, you will see him coming down the road well in advance of his arrival. You will not be deceived by his lies.

2.   Witchcraft not only fosters disobedience to authority in others but *seeks after gifts* instead of the Giver.

Sometimes people seek gifts, rather than seeking God and desire the gifts so they can better serve Him. In essence they are literally selling themselves out for less than God's best. Some believers run here and there, after one big name or another, instead of going directly to

30

God. The motivation of their hearts is in error because they are not seeking the Giver, but only the gift. This can open people to deception of the strongest kinds.

Before I began pastoring in New Iberia, Louisiana I was a tent evangelist. This part of the state had been overrun with unscrupulous tent ministries, one "prophet" even sold his prophecies for a thousand dollars, five thousand dollars, and even ten thousand dollars. This is amazing, but what was even more amazing was how the people believed him and bought their prophecies! These were not stupid people. What was working was the spirit of deception through this "man of God" to dupe the masses. A strong spirit of deception rested on him. After he fleeced the town of thousands upon thousands of dollars, he packed up and went somewhere else. Then the prophecies, of course, did not come to pass and many people were worse off than before. Listen friends, there is a difference between prophesying and *"prophelying"!*

I came along shortly afterward with our tent ministry and the Lord graciously gave us many signs and wonders which helped people no end. A lot of healing occurred in hearts and bodies, and the Lord vindicated genuine tent ministry to many of those who had been previously hurt by the false prophet.

3.   Witchcraft finds fault in pastors, church leaders, and church policies, in order to cause some to take up offenses among the brethren.

If we have legitimate disagreements with pastors, leadership, or church policies, where should it be discussed? It should be discussed with those in governmental leadership.

We previously noted that Elijah built his altar upon the twelve stones, which represent for us today, the governmental authority of the church. Our common sense tells us if there is something wrong, then we should go to the government of the church and not to others. God's government is not democracy, but theocracy. The witch's brew seeks to use the one it has poisoned, to spread more poison among the people.

The congregation needs to be taught, that if anyone comes to them questioning the leadership, the questioner should be **pointed to authority** at once. After all, Jesus taught that whenever one of His followers has ought against his brother, he is to go to his brother. Only if the brother cannot be reasoned with, is someone else to get involved, and then only as a witness. If the problem still cannot be solved, then the offending individual is to be brought before the church and let the church hear it (Matthew 18:15-17). Jesus never instructed anyone to go behind his neighbor's back and spread gossip among the brethren. This is how cliques are formed in the church. Proverbs 6:19 teaches us that one of seven especially detestable sins in the Lord's eyes is:

"... he that soweth discord among brethren."

Whenever others come to you with negative information about fellow believers, you should exhort them that "[love] covers a multitude of sins" (1Peter 4:8). They should be warned against the sin of sowing discord between brethren. This will help them avoid a harmful snare to their own souls. They are being used by the devil, in trying to get the witch's brew over on you. God hates this, and imposes stiff penalties on those who practice such. The Law of God reveals devastating consequences

32

upon those who practice witchcraft (the recurrent penalty was death by stoning!). Thank God we are under grace, but His attitude towards witchcraft has not changed. If you become aware, that you have practiced witchcraft you must repent at once. If it is recent or current, you need to go to those affected by the poison you spewed and ask their forgiveness as well.

Child of God, please heed this warning: if you get into harmony with those who spread discord among the brethren, then whatever chastisement comes upon them for their rebellion towards authority, will also come upon you.

4.   Witchcraft agrees with disenchanted church members instead of defending church authority.

The witch's brew on a person will not let him or her stand up and defend the man or woman of God. It never says something like, "Wait a minute. Now I don't know what went down between you, but there must be a misunderstanding here, because I have known these people too long to believe they could have done what you are suggesting. 'Love believes all things' and I choose to believe the best about my brothers and sisters in the Lord."

You must never allow yourself to get in harmony with that type of thinking. Only by rejecting and repelling the witch's brew, will it not be put on you. You may say, "I did not vocally disagree or reject what was said, but I did not agree with the witch's brew, either. I simply said nothing."

This is the problem. All across America people listen to this junk and think that because they do not agree with the party or take their side they are blameless. *The internal disagreement must be voiced to the poison spreader!* It is proper to not defend yourself when someone comes against you personally, but it is never proper to not voice your support of church leadership. We are obligated to **take a stand for what we believe.**

We believe that the Holy Spirit is working a work in each of us, even though none of us is yet perfect. If you believe that the individual who is being maligned has good motives or that your pastor is doing the very best he or she knows to do, then you are obligated to and and say, "Wait just a minute. I don't want to hear you talk that way about my pastor, elder, deacon, etc."

5.   The witch's brew questions, undermines and finally, judges authority.

When you see judgment passed on authority by a layminister, then you should recognize at once that someone has been taking sips of the witch's brew. Only a general can judge a general. A sergeant should never undermine a general. If a person of lesser authority has a problem with someone who is in greater authority, the person who is agitated has the responsibility before God to appeal to the greater authority with love and a sincere desire to help, not hurt. He also has the right to go to that one's authority and speak his concerns to the one over the individual who is, in the mind of the appealer, operating outside of God's will. Correction always comes from above, never from beneath.

In the final analysis, a witchcraft spirit always seeks to pass judgment on a ministry.

What do I mean by passing judgment? Here are some examples:

34

"I am leaving the church because the pastors are just too busy.

"I don't feel love in this church anymore.

"I am going to go to some other church where people are heard.

"I don't believe the pastor has the right to tell me what to do.

"I don't like the pastor's new policy."

Those who say such things have passed judgment. This is a warning sign for the child of God who is walking circumspectly. When someone passes judgment on leadership, let it serve as a red light signaling you to stop and say, "Just a minute. They are drinking of the witch's brew, and they are trying to get me to drink it too." You should say immediately, "I will not drink of the witch's brew, because I do not want that witch's brew pouring out of you to come into me."

6.   Witchcraft suggests misappropriation of church funds.

"For the love of money is the root of all evil" (1Timothy 6:10).

We have had the witch's brew in our own church. During a recent Sunday morning service we raised a very large sum of money to go towards our new building. There were some people who drank of the witch's brew and were heard to say, "I wonder what they are doing with that money? They have not been talking about that building anymore. I notice that Brother Drew has been quiet since the big fund raiser."

It is important that you realize, friend, that this is a witch's brew and that it is trying to come on you. If a man or woman of God misrepresents the Lord's work and does not use the money of the people of God properly, God, who put that individual there, is big enough to take them out. In fact, He often has!

7.   Witchcraft can work through women, through wives' manipulation of husbands, or through marital relations or social favors.

Sometimes women get offended at something they don't like and begin to suggest things to their husbands that they should not. They create undercurrents in their mates. They even manipulate their husbands by withholding their bodies to help them win their cause. This is a form of witchcraft. The Bible says that a married person's body is not his or her own (1Corinthians 7:4). Every married person should say, "I am married. Therefore, my body is not my own. It belongs to my mate as much as it belongs to me."

A woman should never withhold herself to punish her husband over any disagreement of any kind. Likewise, a husband should render due benevolence to his wife.

8.   Witchcraft rebels against the parental authority.

Let me show you how this works: a married son or daughter receives some correction on an issue from the parent and does not like it. "I'm an adult," they say. Because they are angry at the parent's correction, they

36

refuse to let the grandchildren visit the grandparents. The witch's brew has just been poured. *Witchcraft always seeks to punish and retaliate.* You see, that witch's brew does not like to be put in a place where truth is put on it. Witch's brew does not like authority to tell it anything. Witchcraft is always rooted in rebellion.

When God said, "Honor your father and your mother," He did not say to honor them while you are a child, and dishonor them, when you get older. Whether you are five, or fifty, your mother will always be your mother and your father will always be your father. You are never on equal footing with your parents. God said, "Honor your father and your mother" (Exodus 20:12).

This does not mean we are to always obey our parents after we have formed a new family, since there is a new authority structure within the new unit, but it does mean that we must honor them, respect them, and cherish them. The way you treat your parents could well be the way your grown children will treat you.

9.   Witchcraft promotes a mixed spirit in the church.

A few years ago in North Louisiana a church allowed teenagers to practice rock and roll music in the church basement. The next thing that happened was the church split, and then it split again. One problem after another kept coming up in that church.

The question must be asked, Why? Is it possible that there was a mixed spirit that was being ushered into the church because there was witch's brew being made available to the young people? Are we teaching the young people to listen to anything they want to, at anytime they want to hear it? If we are telling the young people that it is okay at church, then what do you think they will listen to outside the church? Have you ever listened to some of the lyrics of that hard rock music? It is so vulgar that no sensitive Christian can long stand it, that is, if it is even understandable. Things happen at rock and roll concerts beyond the imagination — naked-ness, orgy type scenes, and even urine drinking! If you think I am exaggerating, then I suggest that you check it out for yourself. Rock concerts are nothing but filth and evil.

The same holds true for rock music. You may think there is nothing wrong with the recording itself, but you have no knowledge of what was taking place when that recording was made. Many rock groups speak occult prayers over their albums. Demons are often the "inspiration" behind the lyrics of that music.

Christian, you are either lifting up God with the words you speak, or you are tearing Him down. Jesus said for us to *be either hot or cold* because if we are luke-warm, He will spew us out of His mouth (Revelation 3:15).

Whenever children are rebellious they are suscept-ible to spewing the brew on their siblings and even their parents. Sometimes children get caught up in a spirit of rebellion incited by another sibling. When children mis-behave, and others inform their parents, the parents are frequently "snowed" by their child's insistence of inno-cence. They never believe their own children are at fault and refuse to believe anyone else who comes to them with a report about their child's misbehavior.

A few children are such skillful manipulators that they can always make the parent believe it was **some-body else's fault.** They blame their teachers, other chil-

38

dren, or even their pastors for their own misbehavior. Ushers frequently get blamed by little witches as being mean and unkind, when they were only following the pastor's instructions. Sunday School teachers catch it too. It's always somebody else's fault, but never the fault of the little offender.

Some parents drink of the witch's brew because they would rather ignore the situation than to look at their little darling and to think that they could have some devil motivating them. But God said to call it for what it is. If a tree has many apples on the ground around it, then it is reasonable to assume that it is an apple tree. If someone tells you it is an apple tree, but there are oranges all around, then that person is lying. Don't believe him or her. Confront the wrong fruit!

If a child in the church has a problem with authority one time, I will give him or her the benefit of the doubt. But, when I see a problem with authority here, and another problem with authority there, and a problem somewhere else, then I must deal with it. If the little darling says, "It was not my fault." I reply, "You are not going to put that story on me because your **track record will not back you up.** You have been rebellious to authority, ever since you came here, and I see your track record for what it is. I will not get in harmony with you just because you want me to." Parents, do not partake of the witch's brew!

10.   Witchcraft defends family members above authority.

I want to share one incident which happened in the church which I pastor. Some children were misbehaving and the ushers had to bring correction. When the correction was brought, they went home and said to their parents, "We were not doing anything wrong. The ushers just picked on us. We were not doing a thing. We were behaving." One girl told her mother, "They are always picking on me, Mama, no matter what I do." One set of parents foolishly took sides with the children against the authority of the usher, not realizing that God had placed that usher in his position and had given him authority to help keep order in the house of God.

The ministry of ushering was provided by the Lord to protect, serve, and help everyone in the church. One of their many duties is to make sure that people are able to hear the Word of God. If there is too much disruption caused by passing notes, whispering, giggling, and so forth, the Word of God will not be received properly.

The parents I am referring to. chose to take their children's word over the correcting authority. The witch's brew came upon them. The entire family took offense at our ushers and are not in church anywhere today. Furthermore, the family has been torn up as a result of chastisement, while friends who know them wonder what happened. The problem started right in the church and was apparently over so little a thing as despising an usher's authority.

Mama and Daddy should have instructed their children, "Let me tell you something. That man is a man of God. The pastors have carefully selected fair individuals to serve. They would not bring correction to you, if you did not need it. To be sure you conduct yourself properly in the future, you will sit with us (parents)."

11.   Witchcraft tries to use money to control what is preached from the pulpit.

A dear friend of mine pastors a large church in New Orleans, Louisiana. When his church was first budding, running about 200 people, eight of the leadership decided that they did not like the idea of their pastor preaching the Baptism in the Holy Ghost in the church. They called him on the carpet and told him to preach salvation and even healing, but this business of the Holy Ghost had to stop.

My friend tried to reason with them, but their spokesman stood up and said, "Well, preacher, we are not making it clear enough. You apparently are not understanding us. If you continue to preach the way you have been preaching, we are going to leave the church and take our money with us. When we and our money leave, those doors will close."

At that, my dear brother, with the boldness of the Holy Spirit upon him, stood up and stated, "Now, let me tell you something. Up until now we have had a discussion. But from this point on there is no more discussion. You cannot stay any longer! You must go now, not because you challenged me, but because you challenged God. You said when you leave God cannot keep His church afloat."

The very next Sunday, just to show you how God can work, a visitor came and got saved. As it turned out his one tithe check was more than that of all of the eight families who left the church!

Pastors, I plead with you, *do not allow people to control what is being preached from your pulpit!* Do not let that witch's brew control you. Stand up for what God tells you to preach and God will bring the resources and finances to you. He will sustain you. He is your source and supply (Philippians 4:19). There is no devil big enough to stop you. If God is for you, who can be against you? (Romans 8:31).

12. Witchcraft retaliates through punishment.

I remember a number of years ago a time when some folks left our church. I went to visit them and find out what the problem was. They would never tell me what was wrong. All they told me was, "Pray, brother, and God will show you what the problem is." For two years I tormented my mind with everything in the world. Maybe I had said this wrong; maybe I could have done something differently; maybe something about me needed to be changed. I tore myself apart. I did not have a lot of peace during those two years always wondering, in the back of my mind, what had I done to offend. Then God showed me one day it was a witch's brew.

A witch's brew will many times **leave you where there is no answer**. You will go through something wondering why you can't get any release. It is a tormenting question that has no answer. The witch's brew will torment you and put your mind through hell. You will wonder what you did, when in truth, you did not do anything wrong. The truth is simple: people get angry over irrelevant and unimportant things and allow themselves to be cheated out of many blessings, because of the brew. *Do not let that witch's brew come on you!*

13.　Witchcraft gives ultimatums to authority.

I once encountered an individual who did not like the way we were running a particular department. He did not like the people we had placed in charge of that department. Some of our people did not have degrees, but this individual did have a degree and was upset that someone less qualified in the eyes of the world had been put in authority over the ministry.

One day we were issued an ultimatum: *"Either they go or I go!"* A witch's brew offers ultimatums. I will tell you, without hesitating, we had to make a decision and not compromise what God had shown us.

If you begin to compromise with a witch's spirit, the next thing you know the witch's spirit will control your life. You must do what you know is the right thing to do. Maybe some never earned a degree while others did, but to God, one is just as important as the other. We do not promote in the Kingdom of God by educational degrees. We promote by the anointing of the Holy Spirit. Promoting by degrees is the world's way.

14.　Witchcraft tries to destroy the anointing through sexual violations.

If it can, it will get on the platform through adultery, homosexuality, or perversion. It will try to diminish the anointing. To some ministers the demonic spirit will say, "It's okay to sin, as long as you tell God you're sorry." You may tell God you are sorry for your failure, but if you know in your heart that you will go right back and commit the same sin tomorrow that you did last night,

43

your repentance is false. Sinning unintentionally is one thing. We all fall short of the glory of God. But, you must be genuinely sorry for your sin, if you want God's forgiveness. He will not be mocked by habitual sin. Beware of drinking of the witch's brew!

Whenever a leader commits sexual sins, no matter how secret he is with them, he knows the truth when he stands behind the pulpit.

There is a responsibility that a pastor must recognize. He has to make sure that what comes forth to the congregation is as pure in the Holy Spirit as he can possibly cause it to be. Much prayer must go forth before someone is placed in a position on the platform or in leadership. We have spoken to choir members and our leadership, that if someone has really zapped them and they feel bitterness, unforgiveness, or anger, then they are not to get on the platform. Our choir members understand that they are to sit in the congregation and be ministered to, until they are over it. We have to make sure that what we give is the anointing of the Holy Spirit and not the witch's brew.

God holds us accountable as pastors. Sometimes it may seem like our rules and regulations are a little strict. However, we have an obligation and a responsibility to protect the anointing of the Holy Spirit. Our ushers assist the ministers by keeping things orderly. Someone could distract a person at a strategic moment in his or her life and prevent them from hearing what the Spirit is saying to the church. The Holy Spirit might have pricked their heart and sent them to the altar for salvation had they not been distracted.

15.   Witchcraft uses the supernatural to infiltrate spirits into the church.

Some time back, a pastor of great reputation in our country shared an incident which occurred when he was younger. An evangelist had a reputation for praying for people's teeth with the result that their teeth would be filled with "gold." After the pastor checked the evangelist out, the best that he could, he invited him to his church for a revival. This pastor's wife's teeth were filled with gold during the second week of the revival and people were excited. The pastor, however, began to have an uneasy feeling and bad dreams. The Bible teaches that God will not let anything happen unless He first tells His prophets (Amos 3:7).

The pastor appointed one of his elders to follow the guest evangelist and survey his actions. The elder reported that this minister came out of the motel with a woman that was not his wife. He was later seen taking the same woman to an occult parlor, where he left her while he ministered at the pastor's church.

Upon hearing this report the Pastor immediately stopped the revival. All of the fillings which had supposedly turned to gold returned to their normal substance, including his wife's fillings.

One cannot go by miracles alone. Satan has lying signs and wonders. We have to go by the anointing. Jesus is the Prince of Peace. When Jesus does something, it will leave a peace in your heart. When the devil does something, it will leave you nervous.

16. Witchcraft uses artifacts and plants them on property for purposes of having powerful spirits fight against specific goals.

I recently visited a location where a pastor had suffered two nervous breakdowns. When we began to inquire concerning some of the things which occurred at the time of his breakdowns, I found out that he enjoyed archeological digging. At a certain dig he picked up an artifact which resembled Aladdin's Lamp.

I viewed it carefully and my spirit was very uneasy about it. I asked that brother to tell me what he knew about the history of the lamp. He said that it once belonged in the Temple of Diana and was used to burn incense to that false goddess. I related to him immediately that the artifact was an occult object, and he had brought right into his church, and into his office! That lamp was giving Satan a legal right to attack his mind, causing him to have nervous breakdowns.

We also found out that some time after the pastor discovered the lamp, a mysterious man had come into his church, killed an animal and poured its blood on the altar. That man was later caught and arrested, but they never replaced the altar. God had me advise him to have the altar removed from his church and put in a brand new pulpit. The artifact, I explained, carried a curse with it. Anyone can deny the existence of devils. But, if you believe that there is a God, then you had better believe what God says: there is a God and there is a devil.

Witch's brew comes into the church to manipulate, control, and drive men and women of God out of their minds.

17. Witchcraft gets properties and finances all tied up.

A number of years ago in Shreveport, Louisiana, a beautiful Christian lady inherited a piece of property from her father. It was an apartment complex. It was located in an exclusive area of the city, but for some reason, she could not rent all of the units. Yet, everyone else in the same area had waiting lists. She inquired of me and explained that she did not understand why her units would not rent. She wondered if there was some kind of witchcraft involved. I told her that I was not sure but that Brother Wesley and myself would go over and pray.

After we prayed, Brother Wesley said, "I see Buddha." We went through all of the entire apartments thoroughly and found nothing. So we prayed again. Brother Wesley said, "I don't know why, but I cannot get off of it. Every time we start praying, I keep seeing Buddha." I could have suggested to him that he had missed it, but I have learned that fellow ministers must respect one another. One thing which may help you in any joint-ministry endeavor you undertake, is to realize that if you are working with another Christian, he or she may get something that you have missed. So, I responded to Brother Wesley, "Well, let's look some more. Let's go outside and look around in the yard."

As we went into the backyard, my attention was drawn to a hedge about four feet high. The Spirit quickened me to part the hedge and look behind it. When I moved the hedge apart and viewed its base, what I saw amazed me. A statue of Buddha sat there grinning up at me! Wesley and I grabbed it and broke it in many pieces. (In the Old Testament Gideon and other spiritual leaders broke the idols. They did not merely throw them away.)

The end result was equally amazing. Within just thirty days, all of our friend's units were rented and she soon had a waiting list, just like all the other apartment managers in her area.

Child of God, I am telling you, there could be a witch's brew being practiced on you. When you find out what the devil is up to and put light on him, prosperity can come your way. You may be praying for prosperity, giving your tithes, and offerings, and yet you cannot understand why things don't turn around in your finances. One reason may be that someone is putting a witch's brew on you.

After you find out what it is, where it came from, and break that thing off of you, everything will improve almost overnight.

I was preaching in Mississippi on one occasion when a lady approached me. She could not understand what was happening to her family. She said that they were all born-again, Spirit-filled Christians who loved one another, yet there had never been so much hell and disruption going on in their home as there was at that time. A few days earlier her oldest boy took a knife and threatened to kill his brother. Had the rest of the family not been able to take it away from him, he would have succeeded. There were other problems in the home, too. Sometimes, for no apparent reason, her husband would go crazy on her.

I was impressed to ask her if there was any particular room in the house where these things occurred. She took a double step backwards as she realized that there was, indeed, one certain place where all these strange disturbances had occurred. "These things always occur in the room where the fireplace is!" she said with astonishment. So, I asked her about that room. She replied, come to think of it, there was something strange about this particular room because it always stayed cold. "No matter what we do, we can never can get it warm. Even during summer, it is colder than any other room in the house."

I thought about it a minute and asked her how she acquired the home. She told me that she and her husband made their purchase through a realtor. I inquired further and asked if there was anyone else who had wanted to purchase the property. She replied that, yes, there was a man who had wanted it very much. In fact, after she and her husband bought it, that man came to them and offered to buy it from them at a profit. They refused his generous offer, because they liked their house and wanted to keep it. I asked her if she knew anything about the man. She said he had another house right down the road, with one of those big red hands in front of it because he worked in horoscopes, astrology and fortune telling. I then knew we were dealing with a witchcraft curse on her home, and one that had to be broken in Jesus' Name.

I decided to go to her home and ask the Lord to show me specifically where the problem was. God said to look under the steps. So we moved the cement steps from the back porch that led into the room that was always cold. There, at the base of the steps, was a mojo hand. (A mojo hand is a little bag of herbs, chicken's feet and other things.) The primary idea concerning a mojo hand is to induce witchcraft. It was planted there by that warlock for the purpose of making bad things occur in the home so the family would want to sell their property to the practicing warlock.

We burned the mojo hand. We then broke all of the curses off that property in the mighty Name of Jesus! Next, we went through the house and anointed the doors and windows in the Name of Jesus, reclaiming the property for the Kingdom of God. All at once, Satan's power was broken over that family. They have enjoyed their Lord and His salvation ever since.

18.   Witchcraft violates balance with severe mood swings.

Many times in ministry a pastor is required to make unpopular decisions. I knew a pastor who promoted a member of the congregation to the position of associate pastor and received a lot of flak from other members, including other leaders, because of his decision. Their former mood of joy and support, changed to disapproval and discontent. The spirit of disagreement so influenced his church that the church's progress was slowed to a snail's pace.

The pastor decided he had to address the problem from the pulpit, so one Sunday morning he said, "Some of you do not agree with my decision to promote Brother Bob to the position of Associate Pastor of this church." Turning to Brother Bob, he said, "Bob, will you please stand?" Pastor Bob stood. Then the senior pastor asked, "Would everyone who was led to the Lord by our brother please stand?" Over 300 people, representing nearly a third of the church, stood. The senior pastor then asked a third question, "How could I not promote Bob?" The elders, deacons and some of the other church leaders could be seen lowering their heads in shame. No one else deserved the promotion more than Bob, even if he had not been a member of the congregation as long as some of the other leaders.

19. Witchcraft gives directional prophecy without submitting to the governmental authority of the local church.

If someone prophesies to you and refuses to submit to God's designated authority in that church, do not listen to them. There is your clue. If this is coming from God, one prophet will never mind another prophet listening in. If you are truly a man of God, you will welcome having another prophet of God try your spirit. You must have an attitude of not wanting to give someone a private word, going in a corner and telling them something on the side, which will affect their life. What such people are trying to do, is gain some sort of control over you. People will go and visit other churches and someone will prophesy over them that God is planting them in that place. If you ever receive a prophecy from anyone like that, visiting somewhere for the first time, simply throw it into the garbage. That is not the Lord speaking. Before God will tell you some-thing like that, He will already have done the work of preparation in your heart. If God is moving you from one church to another, it is because He is changing your heart to a different anointing. When someone gives you a prophecy, it should always be a second witness. If God is calling you to go to Africa, you should already be thinking Africa. It should not come to you as a total surprise. You should not have to say, "Oh, can you believe it? Brother Drew said that I am going to be going to Africa. I never even thought about that before." If that were the case, then Brother Drew missed it. Anything that anyone brings in the way of prophecy should be to you a second witness. God should already be dealing with you on the inside.

A Christian chiropractor in our city made it a practice to prophesy over people who came to his office. One of our members came to me distressed over "a word from the Lord" that this man had given her. I advised her to inform the chiropractor that the only way she would receive any future word from him was if he would bring the word he had for her first to her pastor and the elders of her church. He never "prophe-lied" over her again. The Bible teaches us not to lay hands suddenly on any man (1Timothy 5:22). I realize this verse refers to installing officers in the church, but I think it is a good practice to not allow indiscriminate ministry to take place over your life. Keep the witch's brew off of you.

20. Witchcraft uses prophecy to control, manipulate, or impose its will on other people.

We knew a lady in another city over whom a "prophet" said that she was to give a motorcar and $12,000 to him promising that when she did, her husband would return to her. She obeyed the word, but when her marriage was not restored, she became bitter and disillusioned. She quit going to church anywhere and no longer believes in the things of God.

When people say things like, "If you give twelve thousand dollars, God is going to bring this member of your family in," know that it is not God. Anytime there is an exchange of money for spiritual favors, it is snake oil, not the true oil of the Holy Spirit. We do not sell

God! "Your money perish with you because you have thought that the gift of God may be purchased with money" (Acts 8:20).

21. Witchcraft tries to make people more loyal to race, gender, and causes than to the Word of God.

We have seen people of a certain color who want to see their race elevated. There is nothing wrong with this idea except that in order to do this they begin to support people who are pro-abortion, because they are the same color. If anyone is for abortion, they are against God. If you get in agreement with anyone who is against God, then you are casting in your lot with the Antichrist. God is not in the business of killing little babies. God is not in the business of promoting homosexuality. God is not in the business of drugs. God will not allow anyone in authority to stay in authority **in His House**, when they are for candidates who are pro-abortionists. More blood and lives have been lost with babies than in World War II. If you vote for anyone who is pro-abortion, you ask for the witch's brew to come on you. Anything that is against life, is against God. If it is against God, you cannot be for it, no matter what color the skin is. You should not vote because someone is a certain color or party system. You must vote according to moral values, character, and the things they stand for. How much of God do you see in that individual? I am a white man and I see a lot more of God in a lot of black people than I see in a lot of white people. There are many black people welcome in my home. I do not look at the color of the skin, I look at the color of a person's heart.

22. Witchcraft constantly looks for discrimination in the church to talk among the saints and cause division.

This spirit will cause people to discuss discrimination among the saints and will not come and present their issues to the proper authority. It is looking for something that is wrong in the church. They are not treating this group right; they are not treating the women right; they are not treating the color right; there is some discrimination. But they will not go to the leadership and talk about it. This is a witch's brew. If you really feel that your church has discrimination in it, then you need to go to the pastor. And you need to go the elders and the deacons. Then if you cannot get what you need to get, then it is time for you to leave that church. You do not have the right to go to every other brother and sister around you, in your sphere of influence, and say, "Have you noticed, they don't have any of our color in the higher eschalons of ministry." This is a witch's brew. If we are not supposed to vote on the basis of color, then we must never promote on the basis of color. It would be discriminating for anyone to want to remove a person because there are two black people, one playing the piano and the other playing the organ, because there is no white man or woman there, if God sent both of them. We are not to question what God sends the ministry, no matter the color. If you do, then you are drinking of the witch's brew which is spewing out on you.

23. Witchcraft instigates action for someone else to say things or do things on its behalf and then hides in the background as though totally innocent.

The witch's brew will try to get you to do something it does not have the guts to do. It will say, "If I were you, I would give them a piece of my mind. You don't think I would take that off of them, if I were you." When you begin to hear things of this caliber, let something go off in you that there is a witch's brew trying to pour out on you.

24. Witchcraft plants bad seeds through insinuations.

One day a certain woman said to another lady, "You know what I heard? I heard that Sherry and her husband are not getting along too well." Her friend responded, "You don't say! I heard she is shopping for a new husband."

The above conversation did not occur between two unbelievers in some office or workplace. It happened in church!

Not only were these gossiping remarks unfounded and untrue, but they were totally out of character for two Christians to engage in, and completely void of the love of God.

25. The witch's brew tries to suck the life out of the ministers of a church.

It seems that there are some Christians in every church who are always needing prayer, counseling, teaching, and encouragement. No matter how much the pastor helps them, they always need more of his time. Some pastors come to the pulpit weary and unprepared to pour out the Word of God, because they have had all the life sapped out of them by helping one or two people all day.

I call these folks "vampire Christians" because they are always draining the spiritual life out of the leaders in the church, taking up valuable time that the leaders could be using more wisely by helping people who are genuinely sincere. Yes, there are times that people are hurting and need lots of loving input from their pastors, but there are many times that insincere church members unfairly use their pastor's time, even on frivolous matters.

This is not fair to the pastor, to the church he's called to serve, nor to the person who is manipulating his or her time through needless counsel, prayer, and personal teaching. "Vampire Christians" need to be shown the error of their ways and told, in a loving manner, to grow up and not depend on the pastor for everything.

The Golden Keys to Deliverance From the Witch's Brew

We've covered a lot of the identifying characteristics of the witch's brew, now let's talk about the axe that needs to be laid to the root according to Matthew 3:10: "And now also the axe is laid to the root of the trees." I call the seven golden keys of deliverance, "the axe."

What do you do if you feel witchcraft is being practiced against you, your local Church, or someone you love? There are seven ways we can put an axe to the root:

1. Put Light On The Matter (John 1:5).

"And the light shineth in darkness; and the darkness comprehended it not."

The word "comprehended" not only means to perceive or understand, but it also means to receive. Darkness does not receive light and cannot overpower it. Light is always more powerful than darkness.

When our church began to grow and our auditorium became too small, a spirit of dissension began filtering through the congregation: "The church is too big. No one can talk to the pastor now." I addressed this before the church. I explained that it was true that our congregation was growing in numbers, and that it was for this reason we had set in other pastors and counselors, so that everyone could receive proper counsel and help. The spirit of discord soon dissipated.

2. Rebuke It, If Possible (Mark 16:23).

Jesus had to rebuke Peter and say, *"Get thee behind me, Satan."* The witch's brew was spewing out of Peter and Jesus did not hesitate to speak. In Acts 8:20, Peter did not hesitate to rebuke Simon the sorcerer, who had been converted and cursed his money because he was trying to buy the Holy Spirit.

3. Meditate on Psalm 35.

Read this everyday until you break this witchcraft off of you. This particular psalm is especially helpful in the areas of witchcraft and rebellion.

4. Offer Up the Prayer of Agreement (Matthew 18:19).

There is great power in the prayer of agreement. Find someone who is a spiritual person in the Church whom you know is a child of God and carries weight spiritually, preferable someone in leadership. State your business and have them come into agreement with you in prayer. You will have even more power because of the office that they hold.

5. Be Quick To Say To Someone, "I Don't Believe That." or "I Don't Receive That."

If you feel that they are trying to impose their will on you, just be very vocal and let them know you are not in agreement. Don't listen to everything that comes your way.

6. Bring Insinuators/Instigators to Authority (Matthew 18:16).

So, if you have someone who is bringing accusations or insinuations to you, then you bring them to authority. They are trying to instigate a problem in someone else's life, therefore, bring them to authority, where possible. Stop them, and invite them to go to the authority with you to settle the matter. If they refuse, then you should recognize that the witch's brew is trying to spill over on you. What is an instigator? An instigator is the opposite of a peacemaker. Instigators need to be marked and removed from the local church, if they refuse to heed correction and repent.

7. Send Curses Back (Psalm 109:17).

Send curses back to where they came, then bless those that curse you. You may ask how to do this. Simply pray for the individual that curses you, but announce that you do not want the curse they are sending.

The witch's brew will dissolve before any man or woman of God who will stand up against it. Never run from the witch's brew. Be strong! The only way the witch's brew can hurt you, is if you allow it to come on you.

Chapter 5

VIPERS IN THE VINEYARD

Dealing with Dangerous People

Have you ever had to deal with a *dangerous* person? Those who come with guns and knives are obvious, but there are others who are just as dangerous. I am referring, of course, to people operating under the spirit of witchcraft.

The devil will do everything he can do to keep you from learning about witchcraft. He does not want you to obtain any knowledge about it. He knows that witchcraft works best in the dark, and so he wants to keep you in the dark about it.

> [1] *And it came to pass after these things, that Naboth the Jezreelite had a vineyard, which was in Jezreel, hard by the palace of Ahab king of Samaria.*
> [2] *And Ahab spake unto Naboth, saying, Give me thy vineyard, that I may have it for a garden of herbs, because it is near unto my house: and I will give thee for it a better vineyard than it; or, if it seem good to thee, I will give thee the worth of it in money.*
> [3] *And Naboth said to Ahab, The LORD forbid it me, that I should give the inheritance of my fathers unto thee.*

4 And Ahab came into his house heavy and displeased because of the word which Naboth the Jezreelite had spoken to him: for he had said, I will not give thee the inheritance of my fathers. And he laid him down upon his bed, and turned away his face, and would eat no bread.

5 But Jezebel his wife came to him, and said unto him, Why is thy spirit so sad, that thou eatest no bread?

6 And he said unto her, Because I spake unto Naboth the Jezreelite, and said unto him, Give me thy vineyard for money; or else, if it please thee, I will give thee another vineyard for it: and he answered, I will not give thee my vineyard.

7 And Jezebel his wife said unto him, Dost thou now govern the kingdom of Israel? arise, and eat bread, and let thine heart be merry: I will give thee the vineyard of Naboth the Jezreelite.

8 So she wrote letters in Ahab's name, and sealed them with his seal, and sent the letters unto the elders and to the nobles that were in his city, dwelling with Naboth.

9 And she wrote in the letters, saying, Proclaim a fast, and set Naboth on high among the people:...

13 And there came in two men, children of Belial, and sat before him: and the men of Belial witnessed against him, even against Naboth, in the presence of the people, saying, Naboth did blaspheme God and the king. Then they carried him forth out of the city, and stoned him with stones, that he died.

14 Then they sent to Jezebel, saying, Naboth is stoned, and is dead...

17 And the word of the LORD came to Elijah the Tishbite, saying,

18 Arise, go down to meet Ahab king of Israel, which is in Samaria: behold, he is in the vineyard of Naboth, *whither he is gone down to possess it...*

21 Behold, I will bring evil upon thee, and will take away thy posterity, and will cut off from Ahab him that pisseth against the wall, and him that is shut up and left in Israel,...

23 And of Jezebel also spake the LORD saying, The dogs shall eat Jezebel by the wall of Jezreel.

1 Kings 21:1-9, 13-14, 17-18, 21, 23

Each and every one of us come into contact, from time to time, with **dangerous people**, whom I prefer to call *"***vipers in the vineyard**.*"*

I once heard a story about a snake that was going down the highway in the dead of winter. The snake was very cold and hungry as it travelled down the road. A man on the way to the grocery store came along and the snake said to him, "Please, please, pick me up. Please put me in your pocket. Give me a warm place to stay. Please, give me something to eat and I will be your friend forever." The man felt very sorry for the snake, and picking it up, placed it in his pocket. The man continued on his journey and arrived at the store where he purchased his groceries. At the checkout counter he reached into his pocket to pay for his purchase and when he took his hand out of his pocket, the viper was attached to it. It had bitten him. He shook the viper off onto the counter, and said to the snake, "I cannot believe you. It was not but just a few minutes ago, that you were telling me how cold and hungry you were. You promised you would be my friend forever, if I would only feed you and give you a warm place. I did those things and look at you, you bit me!" With a gleam in his eyes, the snake looked at him and said, "Yes, but you knew from the beginning that I was a snake."

Have you ever been set up to be bitten? Is there a snake charming you?

I would like to analyze the history of vipers so you can learn how to recognize and better deal with them.

The first account of the viper appears in Genesis Chapter 3. After God created Adam and Eve and placed them in the Garden (or vineyard). Man was instructed to *dress* and *keep* the Garden (Genesis 2:15). The Garden of Eden was a perfect paradise, but it was right there, in that place of unequaled beauty that the serpent came on the scene. The serpent talked to the woman and posed an interesting question to her, "Yea, hath God said, Ye shall not eat of every tree of the garden?" (Genesis 3:1). How interesting it is to note that this is the *first* question in the Scriptures. Throughout Genesis 1 and 2 only statements appear. The first question in your Bible is not asked by God, or by man, but is asked by the snake.

It is important to realize that a question may often mask doubt. Where doubt begins unbelief eventually results.

Is there a snake setting you up with some of the following questions?

"Hath God said?
"Hath God told you?
"Hath God called you?
"Are you sure this is God?
"Are you sure this is what God wants from you?"

Are you sure? Are you sure? Are you sure? Satan plants seeds of doubt and discord, hoping to get you to miss the mark. After our first parents fell, the Lord dealt with the snake—you will have to deal with the snake, too. You cannot procrastinate about dealing with snakes, i.e., **dangerous people**. You cannot pass the buck to somebody else. You will have to deal with the snake yourself.

> *And the LORD God said unto the serpent, Because thou hast done this, thou art cursed above all cattle, and above every beast of the field; upon thy belly shalt thou go, and dust shalt thou eat all the days of thy life:*
>
> Genesis 3:14

I want to help you understand why Satan is so attracted to you. Have you ever wondered, "Why is he so attracted to me? Why is he always on my case? Why is he always out to get me?" Whether you want to believe it or not, Satan is out to get you because God commanded him to!

> *In the sweat of thy face shalt thou eat bread, till thou return unto the ground; for out of it wast thou taken: for dust thou art, and unto dust shalt thou return.*
>
> Genesis 3:19

God is telling you that the spirit of the devil lacks expression. The serpent seed of the devil, the snakes, the vipers that we face in life, lack expression.

He does not have a body to express himself through, so he looks for an individual, seeking to gain expression through that individual. He wants to enjoy his lower kingdom through that individual. In other words, Satan wants to have a party on your behalf.

The female viper, Jezebel, has become synonymous with witchcraft, wickedness, treachery and spiritual seduction. Jesus, in Revelation 2:20, used the name Jezebel to identify a false prophetess and associated her with immorality and worldiness in the church of Thyatira.

The primary purpose of Jezebel was to do one particular thing. She wanted to uproot the pure worship of Yahweh, and substitute false Baal worship in its place. **The devil is always trying to uproot and substitute!**

The devil is trying to get you to accept something inferior. He wants to get you off course, and to do something that will not benefit you, but will harm you.

Satan intends to do these things but this does not mean that he will be successful. The Bible says:

> *The thief cometh not, but for to steal, and to kill, and to destroy: I am come that they might have life, and that they might have it more abundantly.*
>
> John 10:10

Notice that the thief comes to steal, to kill, and to destroy. Just because he comes against you bent on this agenda does not mean that you have to allow him to accomplish his purpose. *Greater is He that lives in you than he that lives in the world* (see 1John 4:4).

When the devil is attempting to uproot you, recognize these themes:

> *"Have you noticed your mate lately?*
> *"Hath God said?*
> *"She has put on about 35-40 pounds.*
> *"He is going bald as a cue ball.*
> *"All he wants to do is watch television.*
> *"All she does is spend time on the telephone.*
> *"Have you also noticed that attractive person ?*

"Leave that church. You know, really, you have been there long enough.

"You know the pastor's stories better than he knows them.

"Wouldn't it be more fun to go to another church where you could hear fresh and new stories?

"Have you noticed how the folks at the church ignore you?

"I'm telling you, I would not put up with that job.

"They talk to you like you are a dog.

"They don't appreciate your work.

"Maybe that's God's way of telling you it is time to leave that job.

"Are you really sure God wants you to stay in this city?"

Uproot. The devil wants you to consider these thoughts—thoughts that he is sending to your mind.

He will uproot you from your family, your mate, your church, and even your job because this is what he is in the business of doing. This is his purpose. It's all part of stealing, so he can kill and destroy. His job is uprooting and substituting something inferior for something superior—something which God said is real. He will try to get you into the place where he can substitute something less for the best. He is trying to move you and get you to compromise instead of commit.

He is trying to move you into focusing on the gifts more than the Giver. He is trying to get you to look at the New Age instead of the Ancient of Days. He wants you to move off into raw emotionalism or psuedo- intellectualism instead of true spirituality, all for the purpose of substituting an inferior product. He wants you to be

67

lieve you are getting something big. He will make you think the pasture is greener on the other side of the fence…until you get there.

Satan will uproot you and substitute something else in your life for what God wants you to have. God has called you to be something. God wants you to be something. God wants you to stand for what you know He created you to be. God did not make you a second class citizen, or say that you have to settle for second best. **You will never go further in God until you see yourself the way God sees you.** In God's sight you are something special and He wants you to view yourself the way He sees you. You should never substitute your self-image for any image that the devil wants you to see.

The devil will always point out your character flaws, faults, and failures and your lack of knowledge or experience. This is not the voice of God. God always reminds you that you were made in His image. God does not take your negatives and throw them in your face, but God will take your positives and amplify them. God wants you to have His best. **You need to make up your mind that you will never settle for anything less than God's best!**

The Forked Tongued Devil

The devil speaks to us in two ways. The first way is, he speaks to us in our minds. The second way is, he speaks to us through people, dangerous people, who knowingly or unknowingly are tools of the enemy. When you address vipers, those dangerous people in life, you will have to know who you are in Christ. Those dangerous people cannot be overcome except in one way and

68

that is by your personal stand in Christ.

I remember years ago, when I was a young boy, riding down the Airline Highway, before the Interstate was built from Baton Rouge to New Orleans. I always got excited when we drove by a well known snake farm which attracted people from miles around. I couldn't wait because I was always hoping that one day Daddy would stop and let us see those snakes. Well, sure enough, one day after my brother and I had pestered Daddy sufficiently, he stopped and let us check out those snakes.

I was amazed as I watched a python grab a big jack rabbit and swallow it whole. After he swallowed it, he had a big ball in the middle of his stomach.

Do you realize that the devil is trying to swallow you whole?

I noticed that one employee went inside the snake's cage and opened its mouth, pressing the fangs against a glass and milked it, allowing the venom to drip into the glass. I found it very interesting when they told me that they made an antitoxin out of this very venom which could cure you if you got bitten by that variety of snake.

Years later I thought about milking a viper from a spiritual viewpoint. I asked the Lord, "Do you mean that something good can come out of something that was meant for evil?" And the Lord said, "Yes. And so it is with My children."

God is showing you that if you take that devil by the head and press his fangs against the glass and milk that poison into the glass and use it properly, you can use it against the devil. You can take what was meant for evil in your life and you can see God turn it around into something good.

Just because the viper wants to bite you, does not

mean he is going to bite you. Just because he wants to steal, does not mean that he can steal. Just because he wants to kill you, does not mean that he can kill you. Just because he wants to destroy, does not mean that he will destroy. But it is very important that we understand the characteristics and attacks of vipers:

Some Characteristics and Attacks of Vipers

1. When vipers meet they are up to no good.

Conspiracy, treachery, cliques, division. They are breeding separation, divorce, a dislike for the brethren, faultfinding, backbiting, and binding blessings.Vipers focus on negatives, one of their primary delights is running others down.

2. Vipers always justify their position.

Did you notice how Ahab went to Jezebel, his wife, and began to plead his case? "I offered to buy it. I offered to trade it but Naboth is unreasonable. He will not sell me his vineyard. He will not trade with me for another vineyard. Naboth is the one that is unreasonable. It is his fault." Vipers have only one perspective of what is right or wrong—their own.

3. Vipers are only concerned about themselves.

They are concerned only about whatever they want. A viper's conversation is full of I, Me, and Mine. Their focus is self-centered and Narcissistic. Remember Narcissus in Greek Mythology? He was so in love with himself that when he could not stop gazing at his reflection in the water and failed to eat and died. Narcissus was involved only with himself.

When you see an individual all wrapped up in himself, so much so, that he does not have time for others, or those outside his immediate circle, mark him.

4. When vipers gather, it is always for the big setup.

They are looking for a way to get to you. They are trying to find some kind of way to hurt you, some way to take advantage or exact revenge. They want to find a way to try and destroy your confidence in yourself, others, and God. They love to make others feel inferior.

The motive behind all of this, is to set up the object of their denigration.

5. Vipers misuse and abuse authority.

Did you notice that Jezebel went and retrieved her husband's letterhead, seal, and used his name and did all her dirty work? She did not have any respect for her husband, or his authority as king of Israel.

Remember my experience as a boy at the snake farm? One way to render a viper harmless is to milk its poison by pushing it fangs against a glass and "milking" it.

You can take the bite out of the devil by recognizing him for what he is.

6. Vipers love to flatter with their lips.

They will charm you. They say things like:

"What a nice person you are."
"I am so glad God sent you to us."
"This company never operated so well, until you arrived."

But these same people, if they are vipers, will bite

you behind your back, gossip about you, find your every fault and expose them to others. They will look for ways to steal your integrity, or, at least, damage your reputation.

7. Vipers use spiritual things to deceive.

Did you notice when we read the text that Jezebel called a fast? Why? To make it appear to others that stealing Naboth's vineyard was a godly thing. Vipers in the church try to deceive others spiritually. When Satan tries to deceive a church, he comes as "an angel of light" (2 Corinthians 11:14).

If a viper approached you and said, "We are going to kill Naboth," your reply would be, "No way am I going to be a part of that!" But if they come in the name of the Lord, with plenty of prophecies to back them up, it's much harder to discern the true nature of their activities.

Jezebel did not have to wait and think out a plan about Naboth. She knew what she was going to do as soon as weak Ahab whined about the vineyard. A viper already knows what he wants to do to you. He is not waiting for a revelation because he already knows his revelation. He has it planned from the start, and he is looking for ways to set you up and to uproot you from your God-appointed position.

8. Vipers target leaders.

Did you notice how they called **the elders** to a fast? Vipers target the leaders in a church. These "Christian" snakes try to get the leaders to abandon their posts. Snakes will try to get you out of the choir, out of your elder's position, out of your role of leadership, move you from teaching, and move you out of your ministry.

72

Jezebel did not have the courage to kill Naboth herself, but she, through conspiracy and conniving, brought it about as a spiritual thing. She got the leaders of the community to do her dirty work for her.

Vipers not only deceive leaders, but their victims, too. How did she deceive Naboth? She set him on high. You need to be very careful because this is what she did to deceive him. She set him on high by throwing a banquet in his honor. Anytime somebody starts lifting you up, remember, *"Pride goeth before destruction, a haughty spirit before a fall."* When you start hearing flattering words like:

"Oh, Brother, nobody preaches like you.
"Oh, I have never felt an anointing like this.
"When I think about you praying for me, my body shivers.
"Nobody, but you can do it."

Mark them. They are using flattery and setting you up to try to get you into a vulnerable place where the enemy can pull you down. You should tell the individual that it does not matter who is doing the praying, because it is only the Holy Spirit praying through that individual. It is Jesus the Christ who is being lifted up.

9. Vipers charm their victims into a false sense of security.

Naboth attended that banquet thinking that they were going to honor him. He was lulled to sleep. Have you been lulled to sleep? Has the devil put a false sense of security on you? If you are thinking that everything is all right, be careful.

Those of us who live on the Gulf Coast know how hurricanes employ this same deception. When the eye of a hurricane passes over, everything within the eye is under a great calm. When Hurricane Andrew hit the coast, it was as if the storm was completely over — a false sense of security — to all of us in New Iberia, Louisiana. We were in the eye of the storm. And yet, the backlash of that thing was many times worse than what others faced on the front side of Andrew.

The devil, in the same way, tries to get you to relax and let down. He wants you to think that the storm is all over. Lookout! He is trying to get you into a false sense of security so that he can knock your head off. And, like the hurricane, his attack comes from the opposite direction of the last wind. Let me explain.

The hurricane comes one way, but after the eye passes over, it hits in the exact opposite direction. The devil loves to strike when, and where, you are not expecting. If you are accustomed only to frontal attacks, you may be unprepared for a backlash.

10. Vipers get innocent people to do their dirty work.

Vipers tend to be cowardly. They dislike direct confrontation, preferring to instigate, agitate, and infiltrate on the sly. They love throwing out little thoughts hoping that someone will latch on to their innuendoes and suggestions, so they can hook them with some juicy gossip, or slanderous bait, like a fisherman snagging his catch. Once an unaware person takes the bait, they can reel them in.

Are you the victim or the victor? When dealing with vipers one must take a firm stand. Wishy-washy love will not hold up, when you are dealing with a snake, especially if that snake is messing with your children. When children get caught up in subversion, manipulation, or mind games the wise parent nips it in the bud, otherwise, the python will swallow both them and their children whole.

What Do Vipers Want?

Do you realize what the viper wants? He wants two things: sell your vineyard or trade it.

What is a vineyard? It is a place that produces life, harvest, and that from which joy comes, just like the grapes which eventually become wine.

What is *your* vineyard? I will give you a number of spiritual things which you can relate to your vineyard:

Your Birthright

Every child of God has a birthright. Birthrights are promises which Almighty God has made you. The devil wants you to do one of two things: 1) sell God's promise to you or, 2) trade it for something else. He wants you to either sell or trade your soul. *"For what shall it profit a man, if he shall gain the whole world , and loses his own soul?"* (Mark 8:36). The devil will do his best to get you to trade your soul, if he cannot get you to sell it outright. He has caused inestimable suffering and has caused many of God's children to lose out on God's best for themselves.

There is a day of reckoning coming. There is an old saying, "every dog has his day." Satan has his day coming too. I can hardly wait until I see Satan get his day.

Your Integrity

This is another part of your inheritance that the devil wants you to sell. Your integrity is who you really are. It is what you are on the inside, not the outside. You may get bald and fatter as you get older. The outside changes. You do not want your inside to change for the worse, however, but to become stronger and more developed. Your integrity must stay intact for this to happen, so your desire should be to keep your integrity, no matter what. The older you get the stronger your integrity should get. You know what is right. Your mother and your father put those things in you. They taught you right from wrong. You know what you are supposed to do. Your Heavenly Father has put even more integrity in your spirit from the moment He birthed you into His family.

The devil is trying to get you away from what you know in your heart that you are supposed to do. Do it! You know what to do. Do not let the devil talk you out of it. God gave you the capacity to do it. You are big in God. *You can do anything through Christ who strengthens you.* Just do it! Don't talk about it. Do not tell people what you know, do it. Do not discuss it, do it. Do what you know is right on the inside of you.

Get a suitcase and walk up to that rebellious, backbiting, and gossiping child and say to him, "Let me help you pack. If you do not like the rules of the house, then let me help you pack. I am not going to talk to you about it. You think it is better out there. Well just go and have a good look see."

Your Calling and Originality

You may not understand why you are where you are in your life today. You are in the midst of change and do not really understand why. God has you right where you are for a reason. It has to do with your calling and your originality.

I remember how confused I was, when the Lord moved me out of New Orleans, Louisiana, and I could not understand why this happened. I had been attending a wonderful church with excellent teachers and many opportunities to grow and yet God moved me to the state of Texas.

When I realized I was called to preach, I went around trying to find a place to preach. Everyone told me the same thing: "When you get some experience, come back and see us." Well, I thought, how do I get experience, if no one will give me a chance?

A friend invited me to go with him to Newton, Texas, to a black church under the administration of a Bishop named Brother Louis. When I went there that day I thought another minister, Brother Hines, was going to be invited to speak. But when we arrived at this church, they ushered us in, right onto the platform, like some expected guests. Bishop Louis went to the podium and said, "Saints of God, I am so glad that the man that God wants to bring the message has been obedient to show up here today." And then, much to my surprise, instead of calling on Brother Hines, the Bishop looked over at me and pointed his finger at me and said, "Sir, God gave me a dream last night about a red-headed man preaching in this church. Brother, you come take the platform because the service is yours."

The anointing fell. God did miracles. I did not know a whole lot of Word, but I loved the Lord and wanted to serve Him. God will work with you no matter where you are.

Bishop Louis had a God-given love in his heart for me like a son. He took me under his wing for a couple of years. He loved me. He spent time with me. He recognized that there was something special about me in the sense of a call of God upon my life.

One time I wrote Brother Louis a letter of thanks. When he received it, he was suffering from a migraine headache. The pain was so strong that day, that when his wife started to read my letter to him he said, "Honey, my head is hurting so bad I cannot even think. Hand me the letter." He took the letter and shoved it on his head and the headache left.

See, when God blesses, it is always on both ends. The common idea that God blesses everybody else, but I get left out, is not scriptural. When God blesses there is always an **exchange of blessings**.

Under Bishop Louis' tutelage I learned many things about the black culture. I experienced a love birthed into my heart for black people. They received me when, at times, my own race rejected me. I did not understand all of that at the time. As I went on in ministry, after some years, I went back to school and furthered my education. I thought I had finally reached the place where God had given me opportunities now in some of the larger, white churches and I was thankful to God. I found that I was weaning myself away from some of the things that I had learned in my "grass roots" beginning. You see, I had decided, because I was a white man and if I was going to move into my culture and community, I needed to come across with a little more intellectualism and be more what white people thought I should be.

On one occasion I was about to speak at a place that was full of college professors. I remember that night in my prayers, the Lord asked me something that I had to give an answer to. The Lord said, "Why are you ashamed of the gift that I have given you?"

I ask you the same question today. Why are you ashamed of what God has done in your life? Why are you ashamed of the route that He has taken you? No it is not conventional and it is not traditional. It is unique. It is original. It is one of a kind. But aren't you unique, original, and one of a kind? Do you want to be a Memorex of somebody else's experience or do you believe that God knows His business?

I said, "Lord, I don't know what you mean." I lied. I knew exactly what He meant. Have you said the same things to God that you do not understand what He is talking about. I believe you know exactly what God means. It is not that you don't know what the Lord is saying, but that you do not want to hear what God is saying to you.

God said to me, "I brought you to a different culture. You loved that culture. They loved you. They received you. They blessed you. You blessed them, but now you have decided that you do not want to let that culture express itself through you. You have been anointed to *sing-preach*. I gave you that gift, but you will not do it except when you are in that culture. You will not do it in your own culture because you are ashamed of the gift that I gave you."

Oh, I knew I was in trouble! I remember going in front of that church to preach the next day. I do not know how God arranges things, but in that church they had two great sections, one on each side. The whole left side was filled with predominately black brothers and sisters and all of the white, college professors and white folks were on the right side. So, here I was. I knew what God was going to do with me, but I did not like it. (You may not like what God is doing with you right now, either.)

I remember I was going along with my sermon and all my educated brethren were nodding their heads in approval when out of the clear blue, out of my mouth came a low toned humming sound and I sang out, "Well somebody shout Praise the Lord! Somebody say Thank you, Jesus! I'm saved! I'm sanctified! I'm full of the Holy Ghost and I woke up in my right mind!"

The left side of the church with my black brothers and sisters came to life. It was like somebody plugged them into a 220 electrical socket. I heard one brother say, "Come on Preacher, preach!" I heard a sister say, "You're right, come on preach, preach!" We had high church on the left side and no church on the right. The anointing of God fell and everyone was dancing on the left. People were "amening" and some were on the outside - dancing, but they had it going. They had it together.

I glanced over at the right side of the church and rigor mortis had set in. All the professors had their mouths frozen wide open. While I was preaching, these thoughts were hitting my mind: this is your last time here, man, they're going to get you out of here and you will never be back; they are going to mess you up all across the country and you will never get another invite. All of this was going on, while at the same time on the other side, we were having high church. So I just kept on preaching.

Just to show you how God will do something. Out on the right side, a little, white grandmother, about eighty years old, slipped out of the pew. The next thing I knew, her husband followed her, and it hit him. And I noticed that they had something going out there, and then the next thing you know, a few of the other white folks got out of their pews, and they began to let the Lord get on them. I looked at the white, college professors and they were looking at one another. They were looking at what is going on to their right and to their left, and all of a sudden I saw them kind of look up to Glory and ease out of their pew and turned it loose!

I am saying to you that God goes past education, culture, religion, and race. He desires to be worshipped in spirit and in truth. Be real. Do it! Just do it!

Ways to Help You Become the Victor

I would like to give you some points on dealing with vipers, which will insure that you are not the victim but the victor.

1. Tough love is a positive position.

What does the Word say? The Word says, "Honor your father and your mother, as the LORD your God has commanded you, that your days may be prolonged, and that it may go well with you on the land which the LORD your God gives you" (Deuteronomy 5:16 NAS). Father says, "I said 11:00. You go past 11:00, you will be docked by the clock." It is a positive thing when parents give boundaries to children.

2. Mark and avoid known vipers.

Everyone deserves a second chance. Jesus rebuked Peter for allowing Satan to use him, but He did not break fellowship with Peter for that single offense (Matthew 16:23). Good Christians sometimes allow the devil to use them. But when it happens more than once, and it is obvious that someone is up to no good, you need to mark them and avoid them.

3. Ask snakes questions instead of letting them question you.

When was the last time you questioned the devil? When was the last time he asked you a question? When his agents, vipers, question you, you should reply with questions:

> *"Have you talked to them about this?"*
> *"Have you cleared this with Pastor?"*
> *"Have you talked to God about this?"*
> *"Do you think this is what Jesus wants you to do?"*
> *"Let's go see that brother."*
> *"Let's go talk with that sister."*

These questions will help in not letting the devil have his way. Sometimes your silence can be implied consent. Many times you can hear the snake hissing and if you refuse to say anything, you have just agreed with him.

4. Keep snakes on their bellies.

"Upon thy belly shalt thou go" (Genesis 3:14) Why do you think God said this?

When I was at the snake farm, every time the snake would start to coil, the man would take a stick and uncoil him. I asked him why he was doing that. He told me, the snake cannot strike out unless it is coiled up. A snake cannot strike out until it gets off of its belly.

God said he is supposed to be on his belly and it is your job to keep him there. You cannot trample over serpents and scorpions when they are coiled up. Jesus said you will trample on serpents, but the only way you can trample on them is when you have them lying flat on their bellies. If you try to trample on a snake coiled up, he will bite the fire out of you. **Uncoil him**, that is, recognize him for who he is, and what he is trying to do, and put him where he belongs, on his belly.

5. Put great value on free will, authority, conscience, and submission.

In other words, let your character values stand in front of devils. When the serpent is there saying all of his stuff, let your character come up. You might reply with one of the following:

"I do not believe what you are saying about that brother or sister.

"This is a good church.

"I am not going to get into this gossip session.

"I do not receive that in the Name of Jesus.

"I will not think evil of my brother or sister."

Let your character stand up and take your stand!

Chapter 6

ARE YOU A QUESTION OR A STATEMENT?

And the LORD God formed man of dust of the ground and breathed into his nostrils the breath of life and man became a living soul.

Genesis 2:7

Have you been under pressure lately? Are you now undergoing some type of pressure?

Pressure is defined in the dictionary as: *a state of trouble or strain, a compelling force or influence, a need for decisive action.* Do you need to make a decision or some decisive action in your life because of a *pressure* situation that has come on you?

Buck Minster Fuller, one of the many famous inventors of America, once said, *"When I am working on a problem, I never think about beauty. I think only of how to solve the problem, but when I finished, if the solution is not beautiful, I know it is wrong."*

Winston Churchill observed, *"Life is a test and this world is a place of trial."* We, as Christians, can all say amen to Churchill's observation since we have many testings, trials, and pressures.

Pressure is always there. It can make or break a man but God only intended to make men, in fact, He used pressure when He created the first man.

When the Lord God formed man of the dust of the ground the word "formed," as it is used Genesis 2:7, means "made by *pressure*." Therefore, all of mankind started out on this planet by pressure. God never intended for man to stay under pressure, but to come out of it into His ultimate intention.

Throughout the Creation Week God issued statements when He performed His creative work. "Let there be…" He said it, over and over again. When the Creator made man, He made him in His own image and likeness. This meant that He intended man to produce statements, too.

Let's see one way this worked out in Adam's early existence:

> *And out of the ground the LORD God formed every beast of the field and every fowl of the air; and brought them unto Adam to see what he would call them: and whatsoever Adam called every living creature, that was the name thereof.*
>
> Genesis 2:19

Notice that Adam began making statements:

> *...and whatsoever Adam called every creature, that was the name thereof. And Adam gave names to all cattle, and to the fowl of the air, and to every beast of the field...*
>
> Genesis 2:19, 20

It is evident that God never questioned Adam's decisions in giving names to the animals. Every statement Adam made must have made God smile, because He saw His son doing the identical thing that He did: **Adam was making statements.**

In order to further emphasize this truth, let's look at some of God's other statements:

And God said, Let there be light: and there was light.
Genesis 1:3

And God called the light Day, and the darkness He called Night. And the evening and the morning were the first day.
Genesis 1:5

All throughout the first two chapters of the Bible we never find a single question. We only find statements. Keep this fact in mind as we discuss pressure, how God made man to come out of pressure, and what man was originally intended to be. Note that God, in the first two chapters of Genesis, never asked a question, but only issued statements. Then, He creates man in His image and likeness and the man made in His image **only makes statements**, too.

We should also notice that God made one commanding statement which is important for us to observe:

...the LORD God commanded the man, saying, Of every tree of the garden thou mayest freely eat: But of the tree of the knowledge of good and evil, thou shalt not eat of it: for in the day that thou eatest thereof thou shalt surely die.
Genesis 2:16, 17

87

Man had a right and privilege to do anything he wanted to do. He could come and go in the garden as he pleased. He could eat any fruit of any tree that he desired with the exception of one. But concerning this one tree, the *commandment* he was obligated to observe was to not taste the fruit of that tree on the punishment of death.

You Are to Make Statements

When we look at statements in life, we find that we all make statements from time to time. Some statements have great power but other statements are powerless. Why are some of the things we say so powerful, while others simply fall to the ground?

We use them in every aspect of our lives. A salesman will say something one time and it's like boom! It's almost like a revelation and people want to purchase his products. But the same salesman can say something the next day, and it's as if he said nothing.

I have observed the same thing in ministry. At times the people are hanging onto every word being spoken by the minister. At other times the audience is so lethargic, it appears that they are not hearing a word.

How would you like to make statements in your life that would penetrate minds? Would you like to make statements that you know your children are hearing? Do you desire to make statements on your job which cause others to perk up and take notice? Or, perhaps, you have some statements filed away in your heart which you wish you could tell to someone who would actually listen to you?

The First Question

God, in this portion of His Word, uncovers a mystery that helps us immensely. As we have seen, there are no questions asked in Genesis 1 and 2, which naturally leads us to ask a question. When was the first question asked? Where is the first question asked in the Bible? The answer may surprise you, because it was not God who asked the first question. Nor was it man who asked the first question. THE DEVIL ASKED THE FIRST QUESTION!

> *Now the serpent was more subtle than any beast of the field which the LORD God had made. And he said unto the woman Yea hath God said, Ye shall not eat of every tree of the garden?*
>
> Genesis 3:1

Wasn't it interesting when Jesus told the Pharisees that they were of their father, the devil? (Jn 8:44). The word "father" means originator. What a harsh thing for Jesus to say. Jesus was telling those people that the devil was originating their motives and words. The father that Jesus is speaking of, is this devil right here in Scripture who begins to ask questions about God. It was in the Garden of Eden, when Satan began his ever effective method of seducing mankind and getting us to question God.

Do you realize that many people live a lifestyle of questioning God, and do not even realize that they are, in fact, parroting words Satan has seduced them to ask? It begins with doubt and misgivings.

I want to tell you something about the word *ques-*

89

tion. One of the primary definitions of *question* is *a matter of doubt*.

Something happened in the Garden. When our first parents ate that fruit, they exchanged their **statements** for **questions.** They became the product of their exchange. They were filled with questions and became questions also.

You and I, through fallen nature, are a product of our heritage, and we, too, are a combination of both statements and questions. In our natural self we need to understand that our questions are stronger than our statements.

Within any human being who is not a born-again Christian, the questions within that individual are stronger than his or her statements. Why? Because of the Fall and original sin which has passed down upon all the sons of Adam.

If, in fact, the word question actually means *a matter of doubt*, here we see that when a question is posed to Eve, a seed of doubt was planted in her. Satan was inferring something more than the surface meaning of his question when he spoke to her. This devil was inferring that God was holding something back from her, something which was intended to keep her from His highest and best. The devil always infers that God is holding something back from you, when, in fact, God loves His people and wants us to become everything that He intends.

God wants to bless His children coming in and going out. God wants every place that our feet tread upon, to be holy ground and the land of promise, flowing with milk and honey. But there is something that is going to work within our imaginations and thought processes and

90

this something is the devil who is trying to coerce us into a lifestyle of questioning whether God is really for us, and has our best in mind.

Everyone of us have a different scenario, different scenes in life. Some are musicians, others are insurance salesmen, housewives, preachers, choir members, mothers, grandmothers—the list goes on and on. Different scenarios are painted, but regardless of the scene, the base root of the spiritual problem we all have is still the same for us as it was for our first parents. This is the problem—**if** Satan can get us to **doubt** what God says about us, he can control our destiny.

You have a destiny as a child. You have a destiny as a teenager. You have a destiny as a young adult, a middle aged adult, and even as a senior citizen. But if the devil can get you to doubt, he can keep you in check and hold your destiny from coming to fruition. I want to show you some things about the devil, why he orchestrated and originated that first question, and why he endeavors to get us into questioning God's plan and will for our lives. Why Satan wanted man to question, rather than to issue statements. Understanding this will enable us to fight this thing victoriously in our lives.

> *But he must ask in faith nothing wavering. For he that wavereth is like a wave of the sea driven with the wind and tossed. For let not that man think that he shall receive any thing of the Lord.*
>
> James 1:6, 7

"Let not that man…" What man? That man who wavers and doubts. The man who has misgivings. The man who questions God. "Let not that man think that he

91

shall receive anything of the Lord," and then James tells us why:

> A *double-minded man is unstable in all his ways.*
> James 1:8

Allow me to paraphrase it this way, "a man who questions God is unstable in all his ways."

These are some examples of what is thought and spoken by some people.

1. *What did I ever do to deserve this?*
2. *Why was I born this way?*
3. *Is there something wrong with me?*
4. *Why can't I be happy?*
5. *Why do the good die young?*

These are things we say inadvertently, yet they mean a whole lot, in fact, every one of these statements, in one way or another, questions God. Here are some other questions:

6. *Why am I going through this?*
7. *Why is my business not prospering when I am trying so hard?*
8. *Why do I go through this with my children?*
9. *Why is thing held up so long when I have been waiting for it to come in and it seems like it's never going to come in?*

Questions, questions, questions! They never seem to stop barraging our minds, but these are questions not fueled by the Spirit of God, but by the spirit of the devil.

For what purpose? *To get us into double-mindedness.*
None of us ever comes right out and admits, "I do not believe God." You can even ask people who do not know the Lord as their Savior, and even they will admit that they believe God.

Many people who question God, do not realize that they are questioning Him, because deep inside the devil has them wavering. When these people are on a high they will emphatically remark, "My God can do anything! My God can meet all my needs according to His riches in Glory in Christ Jesus! God told me to prosper and be in health as my soul prospers!"

But when they are on a low, and the money is not in the bank, and they are suffering in their bodies, they do not see any breakthrough. They begin to waver. They begin saying the same thing that the serpent said in the Garden of Eden, "Hath God said?..." It comes out this way: "Will I ever prosper? Will my family come in? Will my mate ever get saved? Will I ever be healed?" It is this line of questioning that produces instability. If you must question someone, question yourself, never God.

The Burning Bush

Exodus 3:14 recounts the time Moses saw the bush burning, but not consumed. God spoke to Moses at the burning bush, drew him aside, and told him to take off his shoes because the place where he was standing was holy ground. He gives Moses His purpose: I am going to deliver My children.

Moses, as the discourse continues, replied to God, "Lord, they will need to know Your name, so that they will believe me, when I say You sent me."

From within the burning bush God answers Moses' request: "Here is my statement. I AM THAT I AM. Tell them I AM HATH SENT YOU" (paraphrased).

"AM" is the first person, present singular indicative of the word BE. And when we look up BE, we find that BE means three things:

(1)   Reality
(2)   Existence
(3)   Life.

God is telling Moses, "I Am Reality because I Am Reality. I Am Existence because I Am Existence. I Am Life because I Live."

What He is really saying is, there is no question in Me. There is only statement in Me. I am not wavering. I am not wishy-washy. There is no doubt in Me. There is no unbelief in Me. I make statements. I do not question Myself. I do not have to wonder whether I am really God.

What if God did what we do?

What if God woke up one day and said, "I wonder if I am really God today. I wonder if I can really part the Red Sea. Oh, I did that yesterday, but it looks kind of tough today. I wonder if I was really called to create a man and a woman, looking at what they have already done, all the messes they have made." Of course, God never wakes up and says that because: a) He never sleeps, and, b) He never second-guesses Himself because He is perfect knowledge.

God said all of this to Moses when He told him, "I AM THAT I AM. I AM REAL BECAUSE I AM REAL. I EXIST BECAUSE I EXIST AND I LIVE BECAUSE I

KNOW WHO I AM. It is not a question of who I am, but do *you* know who I Am? Do you know that I am the same yesterday, today and forever?"

Did God bring you this far to leave you? Did God bring you this far to let you go under? Did God bring you this far to let you suffer embarrassment? Did God bring you this far to let you work and work and work only to end up with nothing to show for it? God said to tell His people, "I Am that I Am." He was telling Moses and each of us, "You are a sent one. You are a statement. You are not a question. And your statement is God's statement."

God's Statement About You

God has made a statement about you and your life. You must understand God is not going to change. His mind is unchanged about whatever He said you are.

The devil is working overtime trying to change your mind and get you into areas of doubt and double-mindedness.

Isn't it interesting that James compares this to a ship? He said when you waver, you are like the ship, on the wave of the sea driven by the wind and tossed. In other words, he is saying that when you waver you have no direction. You are out of control. There are many out-of-control Christians, wavering on the sea of life. There are many people who have no direction in their lives anymore. Why are they lacking direction? For one reason. **Because they have begun to move into the question side of themselves, instead of standing on the statement side of themselves.**

The "why's" can drive the sanest person crazy.

Moses delivered the children of Israel out of bondage because he told them, "I Am hath sent me." Moses communicated the thought that God's statement of Reality and Existence in Life had sent Moses to deliver Israel.

Reality, Existence and Life do not dictate that you are to be in bondage. Reality, Existence and Life says you are free. Reality, Existence and Life says whom the son sets free is free indeed. Reality, Existence and Life do not say that you are to be bound by depression, under a taskmaster's whip, under somebody else's thumb. Reality, Existence and Life have something to say and that is that: "I Am" is going to deliver you out of this situation!

The Red Sea

Have you noticed how the question side of man predominated over the statement side of man when Israel reached the Red Sea? It was at this point that the Egyptian forces was hot on their heels. God sent a Pillar of Fire to block the Egyptian's way, but the Israelite's panicked and complained to Moses, "We know why you brought us out. So that these Egyptians can come now and catch us and kill us!" (Exodus 14:10-14, paraphrased). Moses, in response, made a statement, through an action he performed:

> *And Moses stretched forth his hand over the sea; and the LORD caused the sea to go back by a strong east wind all that night and made the sea dry land, and the waters were divided.* Exodus 14:21

96

Today there are other questions and doubts about the miracle at the Red Sea. Some say it was not a miracle at all, because in the year such and such there was only about six inches of water due to the way the tides were moving out. My reply to them is, "Well then we have a greater miracle than the parting of the Red Sea! Because all of Pharaoh's men and his horses drowned in about six inches of water!

Born Again to Make Statements

God wants us to get out of questions and into statements. There is a certain way that we have to maneuver to move into statements.

Notice that God said, *"I Am That I Am."* It appears that Jesus was very concerned about what people thought about Him in this sense. In Cesarea Phillipi Jesus asked His apostles,

> *Tell me. Who do men say that I am?*
>
> Matthew 16:13

Notice the same words, *I Am.* They replied,

> *Some say you are Elijah. Some say you are Jeremiah, one of the Prophets. Some even say you are John the Baptist, raised from the dead.*
>
> Matthew 16:14

Jesus went on to say,

> *Okay, you have told Me what others say about Me, who do you say that I Am?*
>
> Matthew 16:15

Every person who has been born-again has had to make a *statement* to this question. You cannot be born-again, unless you make a statement. People ask me, What does God require in the new birth? I tell them that they have to make a statement concerning the question that Jesus asked, "Who do you say that I Am." You cannot reply, You are religion, You are the Catholic Church, Baptist Church, Methodist Church, or, You are a concept, an idea, or philosophy, a force, or an entity. Men have proposed many different things about the person of Jesus, but only a revelation of Who He is will effect regeneration.

Simon, son of Jonah, received the revelation of Who the Nazarene is: "You are the Christ, the son of the Living God" (Matthew 16:16). Jesus asked the question. Peter made the statement. Jesus then said, "Simon, Bar-Jonah, flesh and blood did not reveal this to you but My Father in Heaven" (Matthew 16:17, paraphrased).

You can never be born-again, until God allows revelation to come to you about His Son. Jesus said there is only one way to the Father, and that is through the Son (see John 14:6). He did not say the Son and His mother or the Son and the church, or the Son and a philosophy, or concept, or denomination. The purpose of the church is to help people get to the place where they can answer Jesus' question when He asked, **"Who do people say that I Am? Who do YOU say that I Am?"**

It is not our place to answer the question for others. Our purpose and job is to help people discover the revelation, so that they can make their own statement.

You may ask me what Jesus means to me today. He means a lot more to me today than He did when I first met Him. But when I first met Him this is what He meant to me. He meant Somebody that I went to that I could not see, but Who I received by faith. I came to this invisible Jesus and remarked to Him, "If You will get me out of this mess, I will give You the rest of my life."

How did He reveal Himself to me? He immediately got me out of the mess that I was in. He let me know just because you cannot see something, does not mean that it is not real. You cannot see the wind, but when Hurricane Andrew rolled through here a few years ago, everyone living here was taught that something you cannot see can be very real.

How was He revealed to me? I began to tell Him other problems I had. I began to deal with stress situations and pressure situations and I came to Him again and said, "Jesus, I believe You are what other people have said You are, and I need a healing. I have been in a hospital fifty (50) days. I have undergone two surgeries. They want to fuse my spine with a third surgery, but Jesus, I heard that You are Christ, the Healer. That You are the same today, as what I read about in the Bible. That miracles did not go away with the Book of Acts...Jesus, the invisible Christ, Whom I have grown to love, will You heal me?" The next thing I knew, my back started improving.

Some people questioned, doubted, and said it was coincidence. Is it a coincidence for around twenty (20) years I have been asking Him for help and He continues to give me all the help I need? Is it a coincidence that every time you get in a bind, He helps you out of it? Is it a coincidence that every time you come to a Red Sea experience, He parts the waters in your life? Is it a coincidence every time you see the lion's den, He stops their mouths? Is it a coincidence when you have to walk in the fiery furnace, that He always either meets you in the fiery furnace, or will take you out of it? Is it a coincidence that He always causes you to walk on the water when you cannot go any other way? Is it a coincidence that He calms your storms?

I would like to reiterate something here. There are a lot of people whom I can see, who have never done for me what another Person Whom I cannot see has done for me. People may say they are your friends, but when you come to them for help, they are looking for an exit to get away as soon as they can.

When I came to Jesus He never told me He'd be praying for me, but couldn't help just now. He never told me He was a little short on funds. He did not tell me that He had problems of His own. He always met my need and did everything that I asked of Him, and came to my rescue when I called on Him.

Therefore, when you tell me that the only person I can count on is the person I can see, I can tell you that the One I have never seen does more for me than every person I ever saw.

Look at what happens to Peter when he makes his statement. He receives the blessing of God. "Blessed are you…" Jesus told him (Matthew 16:17, paraphrased). God brought him to a point where he had to make a statement. But notice his statement was not just his statement. His statement was also God's statement. "My Father which is in heaven" has "revealed it unto you."

The Baptism of Jesus

Let us turn our focus to the banks of the River Jordan. When Jesus came to be baptized, John looked at

Him and said, "Lord, I am the one who needs to be baptized by You." Jesus spoke to John and said, "Suffer it to be so that all righteousness might be fulfilled." So John lowered Jesus under the water. When Jesus came out of the water a dove descended upon Jesus and a voice from Heaven spoke, "This is My Beloved Son." So here is God's statement about Jesus…"My Beloved Son" (see Matthew 3:13-17).

Is it reasonable to paraphrase that what God said, Peter said? I believe it is. Peter made the same statement God made. Is it reasonable to say, that when any human being makes the same statement God makes, then immediately the power of God is there to do a miracle? I believe it is.

Jesus said, in essence, "Understand what's happened to you, Peter! You are not the same Simon Bar-Jonah you used to be. Simon means a reed that sways in the wind. When the wind blows it is like this leaf and it sways hither and thither. You have been called a 'swaying reed.' But you heard from God about who I Am. Because you understand this, I am going to change your name. You will not be called Simon anymore, but you will be called Peter (rock) and upon this 'rock' I will build My church and the gates of hell shall not prevail against it" (Matthew 16:18, paraphrased).

Peter comes from the word *Petros* and it means "a little rock." "Rock" here in that same scripture comes from the word *Petra* which means a "huge rock" like the rock of Gibraltar. What Christ meant was this: Simon, God Almighty, the Rock of Gibraltar has given a statement about who I am. You took your little limited knowledge of that understanding which came by divine revelation and in your own limited way, the only way you could understand it, you became a "little piece" of that "big rock." But you don't have to be a big piece, all you have to be is a little piece. And when you get a statement, a little statement from God's big statement about who I Am, the gates of hell shall not prevail against you!

The devil might tell you, "I am going to have my way in your life," but, if God said something, and if you say what God said, then you become a little statement from the big statement, and the end result is that the gates of hell cannot prevail against you!

When you get out of questioning God and begin to make the same statements God made, there is no devil big enough to stop you or hold you down.

The Sons of Sceva

In the 19th chapter of the Book of Acts we find seven sons of a Jewish Priest called Sceva. They were exorcists. Their livelihood was casting out devils. They came against a big devil and said to the demon, "We command you in the name of Jesus Whom Paul preaches to come out." But the big devil replied, "Jesus I know, and Paul I know; but who are ye?" (Acts 16:15).

Let me paraphrase what the evil spirit said to the exorcists and what the devil says to you: Jesus was a statement, and Paul was a statement, but you are not a statement, you are a question - who are you? You don't even know who you are! You are going to come up to me and try to run me out of this house! You don't even know who you are! You are going to try to rebuke me off —not even knowing who you are! You are going to try and tell me to leave the kids alone and you don't even know who you are! You are going to try and say, get off that job and you don't even know who you are!

This is what happened, because they never had any revelation knowledge, so they could not make a statement. They heard **about the Jesus** whom Paul preached in the same way that people today say, "Mama was a Catholic, so I will be a Catholic." Maybe your mother knew who Jesus was. But, if you get born into religion, you may not even know who He is. And so, you come and say. "I am going to cast you out in the name of the Catholic Church and I am going to cast you out in the name of my Mother," and the devil will say to you, "Your Mother I know, the Catholic Church I know, but who are you?" Because you have never had that personal relationship with God (no statement), you will never have the power to tell the devil anything. Therefore, you would be speaking as though you were one of the sons of Sceva.

Each one of us **must** have that personal experience. You can say, "In the name of Jesus who my husband believes in." He will say, "Jesus I know, your husband I know, who are you?"

You might say, "I command you to turn loose of the finances in the name of Sister Shirley and the Jesus she preaches about." The devil would say to you, "Jesus I know, Shirley I know, but who are you?"

This is the connecting rod between who are you, and what Jesus meant, when He asked, "Who do men say I am - who do you say I am?" Can you recognize the difference between a question and a statement? Can you see the difference between wavering, doubting, not understanding, not knowing, not being a statement and being a statement? Can you see the trouble? Can you see the connecting rod, between what happened to the sons of Sceva and what happened to Adam and Eve?

The sons of Sceva were defeated badly. The Bible says, "they fled out of that house naked and wounded" (Acts 19:17). Some of you are getting *beaten up*. Some of you are trying to cast out devils in the name of something, but you don't even know who you are. You are not doing it because you are walking in the authority of revelation knowledge, but doing it because you saw someone else do it that way. *You are imitating instead of actuating*.

Are You Naked?

What is the first thing that happened to Adam and Eve when they sinned? They looked upon themselves and found themselves to be naked. The seven sons of Sceva wound up naked, because they did not have personal revelation from which issued statements of life and authority.

Anytime you do not know who God is *in a statement form*, but you only know god *in question form*, then you will end up going down the highway spiritually stripped and beaten. And God is saying that He is tired of His children being all bruised and battered and beat up. God does not want His children being depressed, ruled by fear, whining like a little puppy beaten up on the side of the street. He did not plan for His children to come from behind, full of doubts and inhibitions, and misgivings, getting angry at themselves, frustrated and angry at God.

Many people are blaming God for something God did not do. God has given His children power. Jesus said, "I give you all power over the enemy. Any place that you walk upon, you shall put that devil under your feet. Your foot shall tread upon serpents and scorpions and nothing shall in any wise hurt you" (Luke 10:19, paraphrased).

Then somebody says, "I don't know who is beating me up, but you better check somebody, because if it is not the fighter it's the referee. Somebody is beating the heck out of me."

I believe that God is showing us something today and that it is not that the power is not available, but that we have got to get a *statement.*

Make A Decision

This is leading you to a place of decision. God said that when they ate of the forbidden fruit they would die that very day (see Genesis 2:16,17).

Let me submit to you what the death that they experienced was. Death to the human spirit came in the form of division. Up until the time that Adam and Eve ate of the fruit, they knew without a shadow of a doubt that God was. They communed with Him. They had relationship with Him to the degree that Adam even had the mind of God, in naming all the animals. We cannot even memorize them, when they are put in front of us. How would you like to be the one to invent the names for them? Yet Adam did this. How? He had the mind of God. But something happened to Adam. Do you notice that after that there is no account of him naming anything again?

Do you recognize that when death came to Adam, he became a divided person? He became the tree that he ate of. The tree was the knowledge of good and evil. Up until that time Adam and Eve had no knowledge of evil. The only knowledge they had, was the knowledge of God,

105

which was only **good knowledge**. They did not know what evil was. They had only statements in their life. They made statements, because their God was a statement. They did not question things. Everything came to them by divine revelation.

But now, we find that they became divided, fragmented human beings. And the sad part of it is, that death came in the form of a question in the sense that questions began to dominate statements. Adam and Eve became like a ship on the middle of an ocean, tossed here and there and did not know which way to go, with no direction in life. They lost their purpose. They lost their direction.

Cain and Able

When they became confused with more questions than statements, notice what they produced. They produced two children. The first child's name is "Cain." When we look up the meaning of Cain, Cain is a question. The question is *"Can I?"* Cain becomes a question.

Abel is exactly what his name says. He is a statement. But the question came first, which tells us that the fragmented man, was the divided man, that the question now has power over the statement.

Now Cain, the question, comes in this form, "Can I get God to bless me by doing my own thing?" God said the way you are going to do this thing is that you are going to have to offer a blood sacrifice. Cain did not want to do it that way. He wanted to offer the fruit of the ground which had been cursed by God. Cain wanted to offer the fruit of something that was cursed. He asked, "Can I do it my own way?"

What is the New Age philosophy?

You are your own God.
Everybody is God.
We are all gods.
We are all connected to God.
All you need to do is listen to the God in you.

But I want to tell you that it is more than just the God in you. It has to be identification of the Son of God in you. The "I Am" in you cannot be revealed until you know the Son of God.

Now here we find that a war began between the question **Cain** and the statement **Abel**. Abel is a nice fellow, not bothering anyone. I am sure that you can relate to this kind of fellow, not bothering anyone, trying to be a good Christian, a good mother, a good employee, a good employer, whatever. Isn't it strange that the question in life seeks out the statement?

Abel had one problem. Although he was a statement, he was not a born-again statement. He was the product of a fallen nature. His statement had no anointing on it. I do not care, if you are the best man in your parish or county, a benevolent man, kind and a giver of gifts, if you do not know Jesus Christ, you cannot go to heaven. Any statement which man makes without the born-again statement will not have sufficient anointing to see him through.

Abel is making a statement. He is going about his business, doing good and offering sacrifices to God which are accepted by God, but something begins to stir in Question Cain. Cain gets jealous. The question gets jealous of the statement. The question decides that he is go

107

ing to eliminate the statement from planet earth. Cain decides to kill Abel. So Question Cain finds and kills Statement Abel. Abel is dead. Question thinks he has won. There are many individuals thinking they are getting it over on you. There are many who think they can do anything they want to a child of God. I am telling you that the getting over time is just about over with. They will not be able to continue to get over on you, child of God. God is about to call people to accountability.

There is a day of accountability. Everyone will stand before the Lord Jesus Christ and give an accounting for his or her life. God looks up Mr. Question Cain.

Talk about serious trouble, look what happened. God comes to Question Cain and asks, "Where is your brother, Abel? What happened to statement? There was good over there. The tree just did not have evil. It had good and evil. He was good. Although he was not anointed good, he was good. There were good things about him. Where is he?"

Do you think God did not know where he was?

God was trying to redeem Cain. How does God redeem a Question? There is only one way that he can redeem a question and that is to turn it into a statement. You cannot be redeemed by a question. **You can only be redeemed by a statement!**

Simon Peter made a statement, "Thou art the Christ." If he had said, "I don't know for sure, if you are the Christ," Jesus would not have commended him. He could not have given him a new name. He had to know. So notice this, God said to Cain, "Where is your brother? Where is Abel? Where is the statement? Where is the good one? What has happened to him?"

Here is where man gets into big trouble with God.

He refuses to make a statement to God on the question God asks, but instead he turns around and he asks God a question. He replied to God, "Am I my brother's keeper?" Cain failed to make a statement.

God can not save someone if they keep on questioning Him, and they refuse to give a statement to God's question in life. When God asks you a question, **it's time for you to make a statement!**

God had to send Question Cain someplace. The Bible says that when he got through his discourse with God, God sent him to a place called Nod. The Hebrew word Nod means "wondering and wandering," —questioning. All of his life he questioned, and never made a statement. **Cain became a wandering question mark**. He was totally confused.

How many people do you know today, who are confused? Are you confused? Many people in the church today are confused and spend most of their time wondering why. They are confused because God has to show them something and here we have a tremendous mystery revealed to us by God. God wants to change your life. Anytime that you will answer God's question with God's statement, you will be born-again.

You may ask, is there more than one born-again experience? There is one born-again experience for the spirit part of man, but there are "born-again" experiences for every struggle, strain, stress and pressure that you will ever run into in your life. I am saying to you, that there is an answer to you from God, today, right now, as you read this. I am saying to you, that you can become "born-again" even with problem on the job, with problems in the house, with a problem at school, and in any circumstance.

How do I become "born-again" in the trials of life? is the question. When God asks you the question and you give the answer that God requires, you can get "born-again" in any situation of life.

I said earlier that Abel was a good man, but that he did not have power over Cain. The question had power over the answer. That was because his statement was not born-again. But, when we say what God says, God's statement becomes dominant over our question.

Your personal statements do not have dominance over your personal questions, but when you make a statement that is really God's statement, then the anointing comes upon your statement and when the anointing comes, yokes are broken. When the anointing comes, then you can stand against the gates of hell and they cannot prevail against you. When you say about your situation what God says about your situation, it is no longer your fight. The battle is not yours, but the battle is the Lord's. It is not by might, nor by power, but it is by His Spirit.

His Spirit will not come into action because of man's statement, but His Spirit will always come because of His own statement. When God's statement comes out of your lips, you are not fighting the fight any more. Child of God, you are not in the flesh anymore. You are not trying to deal with that devil the way Sceva's sons dealt with him. You are actually saying, "You've got a problem, devil. Don't come looking to me. This is now Jesus' problem."

Prayer

Jesus Christ,
Son of the Living God,
reveal Yourself to my life and situation.

Give me the statement I should make
and I will speak it boldly.

From this day forward
I refuse to be bound by questions,
but I say what God says about me.

For God so loved the world [me] *that He gave His only begotten Son, that whosoever believeth in Him should not perish but have everlasting life.*

Jn 3:16

My statement is this:
JESUS IS THE ANSWER TO MY QUESTION!
Jesus is the solution to my problem.
The battle is not mine but the battle is the Lord's!
Devil, you are in trouble!

In the Mighty Name of Jesus,
AMEN!

ABOUT THE AUTHOR

Drew Rousse is a bishop, author, conference speaker, and Senior Pastor of Faith Cathedral World Outreach Center in New Iberia, Louisiana. This is a vibrant, Holy Ghost church with many denominations represented among its multi-racial membership.

Dr. Rousse is a graduate of Zoe College in Jacksonville, Florida and has been honored with a Doctorate of Divinity from Christian Life School of Theology in Columbus, Georgia. He currently speaks for Christian Life School of Theology, which has over 150 campuses in the United States and abroad.

Dr. Rousse is in demand as a conference speaker and has ministered in conventions throughout the United States and overseas. He has an anointing to change churches by teaching and ministering deliverance in a balanced, sensible way.

Drew has been on daily radio since 1980 and co-hosts a weekly 30 minute television program along with his wife. *The Drew and Wanda Rousse Program* has been on the air in South Louisiana since 1987. Wanda is a gifted minister in her own right and joyfully assists her husband in achieving his highest and best for God's glory.

Noted ministers such as Charles Green, Jerry B. Walker, Ron Cottle, and Herro Blair highly recommend Dr. Rousse. For more information on books, tapes and videos, or to invite the Rousses for speaking engagements, call (337) 367-7223, contact *www.drewandwanda.org,* or write:

Faith Cathedral Ministries
PO Drawer 9380
New Iberia, LA 70562-9380

BOOKS AND TAPES
BY DR. DREW ROUSSE

Ordering Procedures

Please send your request with a check or money order made out in US dollars and mail to:

Faith Cathedral
P. O. Drawer 9380
New Iberia, LA   70562

Foreign orders – please note:
Checks must be made payable in US dollars

TAPE SEMINARS

Each tape seminar includes 10 hours of college level teaching on cassette, a syllabus and a textbook.

QUANTITY   TITLE   DONATION

_____   *Advanced Deliverance I* $50.00
A study of the deliverance ministry from a practical viewpoint

_____   *Advanced Deliverance II* $50.00
Teaching on deliverance principles and patterns from the book of Genesis

_____   *How to Hear the Voice of God* $50.00
Teaching on the many ways God speaks to us

_____   *Deliverance Workshop* $50.00
Practical applications for effective ministry in the area of deliverance

THREE TAPE SERIES

QUANTITY	TITLE	DONATION

_____ ***2001: A Speech Odyssey*** $15.00
The Rhema moments of life require positive voice activation. Learn what to say, and when to say it.

_____ ***Are you ...?*** $15.00
Saved, Sanctified, Full of the Holy Ghost

_____ ***Battling the Hosts of Hell*** $15.00
Develop a battle plan for spiritual wars.

_____ ***The Battle is the Lord's*** $15.00
The right prayer at the right time produces the right results

_____ ***Break Through*** $15.00
Break witchcraft, soul ties, and hear the sound of rain

_____ ***The Elusive Butterfly*** $15.00
It is possible to be perfect in an imperfect world

_____ ***Dealing with the Devil*** $15.00
If we know what he's up to, it helps us be spiritually efffective

_____ ***Emotionally Charged Memories*** $15.00
De-charging the traumas of life

_____ ***Fight to the Finish*** $15.00
Apostle Paul's secrets to Victory!

_____ ***Gerizim*** $15.00
What you say, and when you say it, hold the keys to life and death

_____ ***Getting Your Family Saved*** $15.00
Messages geared specifically to bringing your loved ones into the Kingdom of God.

_____ ***Hayah*** $15.00
The revelation of "I AM" and what it means

_____ ***In the Midst*** $15.00
Involve Jesus in every aspect of your life.

THREE TAPE SERIES (Cont'd)

QUANTITY	TITLE	DONATION

_____ **_Make Me Whole_** $15.00
What your daddy told you has impacted your life.
_____ **_Moving On Up_** $15.00
Spiritual promotion and how to attain it
_____ **_Ready to Rumble_** $15.00
Spiritual Secrets to fight the good fight of faith
_____ **_Stress_** $15.00
Evaluate, eliminate, and stress-proof yourself.
_____ **_True Worship_** $15.00
Worship includes everything even TRIALS
_____ **_Witchcraft_** $15.00
Identification of territorial demons who are net-
working against you.
_____ **_Witch's Brew_** $15.00
Is someone practicing witchcraft on you?

Please send my order to the following address:

Name:_____

Address:_____

City:_____

State : _____   Zip:_____

[   ]   I would like to become a Jesus Power Partner. My
$15.00 **monthly** love gift to Faith Cathedral ensures that I
will receive a cassette of Dr. Rousse's most anointed message each month.

POWERFUL NEW BOOK

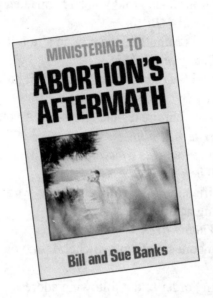

This new book is unique because it offers real help for the suffering women who have already had abortions. This book is full of GOOD NEWS!

It shows how to minister to them, or may be used by the women themselves as it contains simple steps to self-ministry.

Millions of women **have had abortions**: every one of them is a potential candidate for the type of ministry presented in this book. Every minister, every counsellor, every Christian should be familiar with these truths which can set people free.

$5.95 + $1.50 Shipping/Handling

Impact Christian Books, Inc.
332 Leffingwell Avenue, Suite 101
Kirkwood, MO 63122